The Will To Survive

Brendan McLoughlin

BLACKWATER PRESS

ACKNOWLEDGMENTS

Dr. Conor Burke and all the dedicated nurses and staff of James Connolly Memorial Hospital. Mr. Dark, the transplant surgeon and all the team at the Freeman Hospital, Newcastle-upon-Tyne. Dr. Bell and all the people who looked after me in Donegal and Sligo. The media, President Mary Robinson and all my well-wishers. My special friends Martine Brangan and Martin Byrne.

Editor: Brenda McNally
Design & Layout: Paula Byrne
© **1993** Blackwater Press,
Broomhill Business Park, Tallaght, Dublin 24
ISBN: 0 86121 4986

Dedication

*'To my mother (to whom I owe my life)
and all those whose lives are touched with the hope of a
life-giving transplant.'*

CONTENTS

Foreword 1

1 In The Beginning 4

2 Learning To Survive 8

3 Goodbye School 13

4 Birds Of A Feather 20

5 Jingle Bells 25

6 The Will To Survive 31

7 Young And Not So Carefree 36

8 Taking Heart 41

9 An Ill Wind 47

10 A Glow Of Limelight 55

11 August Weekend 1991 62

12 The Sky Is Not The Limit 70

13 Losses and Gains 91

14 Now and Forever 104

15 Fit to Survive 109

Epilogue 115

Afterword 141

FOREWORD

I remember the day my second child, Brendan was born. On the beautiful spring morning of 17th May, 1967, I was awoken by the labour pains. The sun was rising, I felt calm and unhurried, quite full of joy and confidence at the prospect of the birth. Taking things in my stride, I got on with the task of getting my first born, Gerard, ready to go to a neighbour's house to be looked after. It never entered my mind that the baby who was about to make its appearance would be anything but a normal healthy child.

Brendan was in a hurry to see the world outside. I travelled the fifteen miles to Letterkenny Hospital by taxi, in the company of my sister-in-law and a neighbour who was a nurse. It could have happened at any moment along the journey. Still, I was in good company, and as things came to pass my son was born before I got to the delivery room. But after the birth he didn't cry; the medical staff hurriedly untwisted the umbilical cord from around his neck and as he finally uttered his first little wail I thought all was well, no more problems. I had a fine little lad of 8lbs., 4oz.

After that day, the long, hard struggle began as Brendan started to cry and cry and cry. He never stopped, day or night. I took him home from the hospital as there didn't seem to be anything definitely wrong with him apart from his incessant crying. Then a chronic bowel blockage followed, and vomiting. He was constantly sweating and a little cough developed which never went away. Now I began to worry, and sought to have him investigated. It was years before I got any definite answer about his trouble, and that was when he came under the care of Dr. Bell. I had gone through wondering whether it was asthma or bronchitis, and now the name given was cystic fibrosis. As time went on the name of his disease changed and confused me, but now I am assured that the original diagnosis was the correct one.

I often wondered what the future would bring as every day a different problem had to be mastered. At mealtimes he was always sick at the table, so I had to train my other children to learn to live with that and anything else that might happen. But I made it my rule to treat Brendan just like his brothers and sisters.

There were so many trying voyages through the journey of his life, some very difficult to overcome. I loved him so very much that it was heartbreaking to see him suffer as he did, and still does. At night, if I did not hear him coughing I was nearly afraid to look in on him, in case he'd passed away. When I was separated from him, while he was in hospital, I was always waiting for bad news. My heart used to miss a beat whenever the phone rang; I lived in fear of losing him.

As the years went by he deteriorated badly, but always during a crisis I got a flash in my mind that he had to make it with God's help. On my last visit to see him in a Dublin hospital I saw such a change in him that I just wanted to pick him up in my arms and take him home with me. I had been notified that he was critical and I feared that he might be gone before I could make the two-hundred mile journey from Donegal. That was the most distressing time in my life. After twenty-four years of caring for him, I thought that I might not be there when he needed me most. I can never get used to the idea that I could lose him.

Brendan is now waiting for a lung transplant, and I hope and pray each day that he will soon get the operation that might give him the chance he deserves of comfortable health. He is a gentle, kind, trusting and loving boy with a passion for living. He gets so much joy out of life and the people he meets. I trust that God will have chosen him and that He will guide the surgeons' hands during the operation. I would not want any mother to go through what I have gone through, only the love of Brendan made it all possible. May God give him the strength to go on.

There are many, many people I am indebted to for helping us through the difficult times, including doctors, nurses, orderlies, physiotherapists, kitchen staff, porters, fellow patients, priests, neighbours, ambulance drivers, the media, social workers; in fact anybody who played a part in Brendan's survival. I don't intend taking up too much of this book in naming everyone individually, but I must give particular mention to our very special friends: Sarah McNulty, a very good and holy person from our home town of Ballybofey has supported us throughout in thought, prayer and deed; and for Martin Byrne and Martine Brangan, my ears and eyes in Dublin, I have nothing but praise. They have stayed by Brendan in Dublin, proving that nothing was too much trouble for them.

God Bless All And Look After Them.

FRANCES McLOUGHLIN
(May 1992 – in hope of a
transplant for Brendan)

1
—

IN THE BEGINNING

You can go no further north in Ireland than Malin Head, in county Donegal. When a gale is blowing across the headland you can hear an orchestra, the sound of the sea, the mighty Atlantic Ocean as it hurls its thundering waves mercilessly against the jagged rocks and yellow ochre sands of this promontory. Muted tones of every season greet the visitor's eye: a whole spectrum roughly jigsawed together, with sapphire and rose mountains and myriad fields of every colour in an artist's paintbox.

In times still spoken of, passenger boats would arrive to nearby Moville from Glasgow in Scotland. A traveller alighting from this vessel would be introduced to this most individual county in the land of Ireland. The boat service no longer exists , but has for some time been replaced by an airlink. On a clear day, you can see across to the Inner Hebrides of Scotland. Donegal could be described as the forgotten corner of Ireland being linked as it is to the twenty-five remaining counties by a mere bottleneck of land. Most of the county borders with Northern Ireland.

I have yet to see much of my beautiful Donegal, owing to travel restrictions imposed thus far by a life of ill health. Presently, I keep my fingers crossed that my life will soon be transformed; that I may have the freedom to explore within and beyond the confines of my native county. We have been described as an observant, strong willed people. As an essentially Donegal man, I would choose the word stubborn as perhaps the most apt. If there's something that needs to be done, we'll notice it and we'll do it. I see in my neighbours, my family and myself a strong sense of perseverance. It is this characteristic which has fed my will to survive.

My birthplace is Carn, not exactly a village, but a scattering of dwellings near the town of Ballybofey, in the heart of Donegal. The second eldest in a family of six, I was born on the seventeenth day of May, 1967. My parents were not well off and had to rear their children in a small, decaying cottage. One of my three brothers and my two sisters also were prone to chest complaints which were not compatible with our living environment. Fortunately, their health remains reasonably good, although my sisters were both recently diagnosed as having my disease too. My respiratory troubles however, proved to be more severe, and only recently was the diagnosis of cystic fibrosis (C.F.) confirmed. I have reached a stage where my illness is terminal; my only hope of avoiding death lies in the chance of receiving a new lung.

My mother tells me I had quite a few problems at birth, despite weighing a healthy 8lbs., 4oz. There were breathing difficulties, I was noticeably cyanosed and short of oxygen, and I sweated considerably. I developed an irritating cough which tended to induce vomiting. This meant that I got little benefit from the feeding I was given and so I failed to gain weight like the average baby. My constant crying troubled my mother to the extent that she occasionally resorted to giving me the odd drop of whiskey in the hope that I might sleep a little better.

The first occasion of dramatic illness began when I developed convulsions, whereupon I was rushed to Letterkenny General Hospital. I was eight-months-old at the time. There I remained in a critical condition for three days, having caught pneumonia. My parents were contacted as there was doubt about my surviving the illness. A priest was sent for, and he administered the sacraments. It was touch and go for a while, but eventually I recovered sufficiently to be sent home.

Healthy children can be a trial and worry to their parents, but a young child with considerable ill health, such as I had, demands extra care. A good friend by the name of Fr. McKee, a local Catholic priest, grew concerned about my mother not getting enough sleep. He stepped in to give her a break and got first-hand experience of the difficulties that beset her. The poor man walked the floors with me, thinking it rare that I would not stop crying, no matter what he did. He tried giving me a soother, but I couldn't take it because I was inclined to smother on it. I'll bet Fr. Mc Kee thanked God he didn't have this difficult child for keeps!

My mother had to look after all my needs with no support from my father, who was falling prey to alcoholism. Among the things that necessitated her attention was a stubborn form of constipation which affected my weak digestive system. As my bowel would not function of it's own accord she used the old-fashioned, plain soap remedy to keep things moving in the right direction. This might have to be done up to three times daily. Little did she know at this early stage how many more medical routines she would have to perform in the years that lay ahead.

Good Friday is celebrated as the day Jesus Christ was crucified, an important day in the Roman Catholic calendar. On this day, shops, banks and post offices, all close their doors and the town of Ballybofey, like everywhere else in Ireland, comes to a standstill. It was on one such Good Friday that my mother decided to clean the range. It was a big old iron affair which, using solid fuels, was a cooker and a heater in one. She put a kettle full of scalding water on the floor and proceeded to clean. My older brother, Gerard, and I were playing in the room and in the excitement of the pushing and shoving I fell on the kettle. I was two-and-a-half years old so the scalding I received covered most of my bottom quarters, including my private parts. This is a serious enough accident for any child to encounter, but my mother was especially worried about the consequences it could have on me. Good Friday was not the easiest day to locate a doctor in the countryside so it was evening time before one arrived. He treated the huge blisters which had formed, but did not consider it necessary to send me to hospital. I was in agony and could not bear to be touched for days, giving my long-suffering mother a nightmare of a nursing job.

When I was three-years-old I started to learn to walk without support from adult hands. A milestone for any child and a relief for my mother who was beginning to wonder if I would ever walk at all. Every time I had made any progress towards learning, a lung infection would set me back so that walking, which was old news for most three-year-olds was a new experience for me. Progress was also halted by fluid building up on my joints which, without passive exercise could have confined me to a wheelchair. However, the daily physiotherapy administered by my ever-patient mother meant progress was a little late, as opposed to never. Now, as an adult man, my limbs are quite mobile, but my lungs haven't the puff to carry me very far, so during my infancy, mother was instructed to commence physiotherapy for my lungs. To this day she is still doing this for me, both of us fighting my battle to survive.

2
—

LEARNING TO SURVIVE

For many years I lead a life that was not too different from that of the other young boys, although I was a very sickly child. At school I was more interested in getting up to mischief than in learning my lessons, but with my look of innocence I got away with murder. I remember one occasion when some friends and I were playing near the road and thought it would be fun to throw stones at passing cars. Caring little about any possible damage to property, we gleefully hurled our missiles, laughing at the fury of the car drivers! Our fun turned somewhat sour when a stone thrown by me actually broke a window. We hadn't intended it to go that far, and terrified, ran from the scene of the crime, back to school where we belonged.

By the time we reached the school we had regained our slightly warped sense of humour and were in high spirits as we sauntered through the gates. But we stopped dead in our tracks. There in front of us was a teacher's car, with its window smashed! No one suspected that yours truly, the blue-eyed boy, was involved.

Perhaps luckily for the car owners in the school, my education became very disrupted at this point. I was rushed to Letterkenny General Hospital, blue light flashing and siren wailing when I began coughing up blood. I was only ten-years-old at the time and remember feeling a mixture of terror that I was going to die and elation at being so important as to be the passenger in an emergency ambulance. However my excitement soon turned to boredom as the medics began a long examination. It was discovered that I had a very high fever and badly congested lungs. My condition gave cause for concern, especially to my mother who, having a large family to attend to, was forced to take the bus fifteen lonely miles home to Ballybofey. For my part, I was distracted by my surroundings and wasn't all that worried about my lungs.

So began my lifelong relationship with hospitals, and their staff. My body-clock soon adjusted itself to the rythyms of 'hospital time' with its 6.00 a.m. awakenings and early bedtimes. I became familiar with medical terms: diseases of the lungs were 'pulmonary', those which ran in families were 'hereditary', a P.F.T. was a 'pulmonary function test' and an I.V. was an 'intra-venous', and it hurt.

It was during this stay at hospital that I first met Dr. Bell, a consultant paediatrician from Sligo General Hospital. Having conducted an examination, he decided to take me with him to Sligo for further investigation. To her dismay, Mother was notified of this decision and I was transported much further from home in order to get to the roots of my problem. As the ambulance drew into the courtyard of Sligo General, my first thoughts were that they had taken a wrong turn and brought us to a prison. The old austere grey walls with their narrow windows were in fact the hospital. It struck me as the kind of place you go into but never come out of. However, I was happy to discover that the paediatric unit where I was to stay was located in a less antediluvian part of the hospital complex. Obviously, someone who had remembered their own childhood was responsible for the cheerful decor. The walls were various pastel shades, and colourful cut-outs of Mickey Mouse and his many pals smiled out from every corner. It seemed very pleasant in contrast to my first impressions of the outside.

I remember my first experience of student doctors at this time. They followed behind the consultant like chicks after a hen, and seemed to want to outdo each other with their questioning. I recall enjoying the attention immensely, as they were told that, at present I was functioning on a quarter of my lung capacity and that I had been given this treatment, and that treatment and was now under investigation for cystic fibrosis. I was, they were told, very prone to infections, needing regular courses of antibiotics which, on that occasion, needed changing, as they did not seem to be winning any battles with the germs.

When the students had finished asking every question you could think of they trotted off after mother hen and I was left to consider my next move. I was and still am a television addict, it doesn't take a lot of energy to sit in front of one, so it suited me fine. I headed for the dayroom as this was where the television had been in Letterkenny General. No sooner had I begun viewing a good murder film, when I dozed off; it had been a long day and I was escorted back to bed.

Another 6.00 a.m. awakening. It was explained to me that the night nurses were going off duty and it was their responsibility to give the first medication. It kind of made sense; breakfast arrived at eight by which time I thought it was about midday and was ravenous. I ate and then looked for distractions for the day. Television ... I headed for the day room only to be headed off by a lady doctor, "Are you Brendan?", "I am." "Then come along with me please, we have a test to do."

I had blood tests which produced little labelled bottles to be sent to the laboratory and I had X-rays which produced pictures of my chest for Dr. Bell. Looking at them, it was hard to believe that those were actually my ribs on the plastic photos. I was assured that they were and that they would help in my treatment. In a children's department all procedures are carried out privately in a special 'treatment room', so as to prevent any of the other little patients from witnessing anybody else's distressing moments.

My main interest, though an enforced one, has been medicine. From my earliest admissions to hospital, my brain has been buzzing: always seeking answers, wanting to know the whys and wherefores. Every test, chart and procedure had to be scrutinised and assimilated. Every doctor and nurse had to be quizzed, evaluated and weighed up. I wanted to be the expert on me and on my condition. I wanted to know my medical history and plan my medical future. I believe that a patient should know all that there is to know about their illness. Far too often, patients lie in bed whilst doctors play tennis over their heads with medical jargon. The irony is that in spite of having such an insatiable curiosity about my own condition, I have been repeatedly confused and led astray by the different diagnoses and changes in treatment I have been given over the years. The first definition of my illness was cystic fibrosis; in later years a couple of different names were used to describe my condition, and only recently I have learned that the first diagnosis was the correct one.

Sligo town, where the hospital is located, is over fifty miles from Ballybofey. Being such a distance from home meant that I received only the occasional visit from my mother and family. We could not afford the expense of a car, nor that of several long distance bus fares, and there was no telephone in our home which added to the inconvenience and lack of easy communication. In spite of this, Mother made the best possible efforts to come and see me, keeping in touch with my progress via the nearest public phone which was over a mile away in the town.

During this time Mother took pity on a very ill, handicapped young baby who had been abandoned by its mother for reasons unknown. On each visit to me she would also spend some moments with the little infant, almost becoming the mother it never had. One day the baby was no longer there, it had died during the night. To this day my mother speaks of the grief she felt, as though it had been one of her own children.

For long-stay young patients who would otherwise miss out on a considerable amount of schooling, an education service is provided by a visiting teacher. Like every 'non-medical' activity this would take placc in the dayroom. For the allocated time, non-pupils would be excluded from watching television or playing games in the improvised classroom. Here I had to behave myself just as if I was at my local national school in Ballybofey. A noticeable difference was that there was no blackboard. In consideration of the varying ages, standards, and attention spans of the sick pupils, individual attention was the basis of the teaching practice.

Three weeks seemed to be three years, but finally I was released from Sligo General. I had never been separated from my family for so long and, mixed with my delight at seeing them all again was a feeling that I would know many such separations in the time ahead.

3
—

GOODBYE SCHOOL

During the later years of my childhood my life style began changing significantly. The investigations and test results seemed to puzzle the doctors. I was treated for the infections which were destroying my lungs, with large doses of antibiotics. In school I was picking up infections that other children brought in with them, and developing complications which landed me in hospital all too often. The journey from home to the classroom involved a long uphill walk through damp fields and eventually I just was not able for it. The first thing I would do on arrival was cough my lungs out and vomit. If I could make it to the bathroom in time, then nobody else had to witness the scenario. There was nothing for it but to wave goodbye to school. At the tender age of eleven my formal education ceased.

I say 'formal' because my education was not forgotten. My mother adopted another role alongside that of nurse, housekeeper, cook and counsellor; she became my teacher. Not forgetting that she had a hundred other duties to occupy her, especially now that the youngest member of the family, Martina, was just a few months old. Between changing nappies and giving my baby sister her feeds, Mother would have to check my written work and assign new exercises. This was a formidable task for her because she herself had received little enough education. She had to re-learn what was distant in her memory from her own schooldays, and absorb new material from the recommended textbooks. I am told that I was a difficult pupil, and it was hard work to get me to learn what was necessary. I would be distracted like most young pupils, by anything other than lessons. However, the determination of a mother that her ailing son should learn to read and write won through and I was schooled at home.

Within two months, I was back at Sligo General with a congested lung. I was in the adults' ward for a few days to start with and remember being extremely bored. There was no-one near my own age and I was surrounded by older men in a functional looking ward. Not what the budding teenager calls fun I can assure you. I was thrilled when at last I took up residence in the childrens' ward amongst those I could relate to.

People say I could talk to anyone; I made friends quickly and soon we children were the loudest things in the hospital, playing jokes on the nurses and any student doctor unlucky enough to cross our path. It was here that I met my partner in crime, Thomas Mc Gomery, a Donegal lad and extrovert like myself, a bit of a wild fellow in fact and the master of some marvellous mischief. He was liked by everyone including my mother who said after a lively visit, that I had met my match. We were to meet many times in the following years and had some great fun.

It was suggested to my mother and I that cystic fibrosis might well be the causative agent of all my symptoms, from the repeated chest infections to the nausea, intestinal colic, constipation and occasional diarrhoea that I was inclined towards. This disease affects all mucus secreting glands of the body, whereby they produce fluid which is much thicker, more gelatinous and less free-flowing than normal. The digestive juices are prevented from reaching food properly, resulting in poor nutrition and bowel disorders, but the most troublesome and incurable problem affects the lungs, where difficulties arising from fluid build-up gradually destroy the vital breathing apparatus.

A small machine was attached to my arm by swabs which collected sweat; these were left in place for about ten minutes, after which they were sent to the lab for analysis. Results with an abnormally high salt content indicated that I had cystic fibrosis. Dr. Bell put me on 'Cotazym B' tablets which replaced the digestive enzymes that were absent in my system, and this eased some of my symptoms appreciably.

The only two days that were worth giving a name to in hospital were Sunday and Tuesday. Sunday, although monumentally boring for a would-be active teenager, at least individualised itself by having a Mass and fewer routines. Tuesday was visiting day for me. Mother would arrive on the bus from Ballybofey and we would spend the day exchanging news. She told me about the latest family doings and undoings. I would fill her in on my progress, if I wasn't happy with anything she could be very vociferous about putting it right! That was the best day of the week, reminding me that I was part of a family with a life, not just a patient in another anonymous hospital bed.

The staff at Sligo General knew how monotonous things could be for myself and Thomas in hospital during the summer months; they knew because when we got bored between routines and schooling, we got restless and when we got restless we got into trouble. So it was that two of the hospital staff, a doctor and a porter decided to take us with them on a sight-seeing tour they had planned one sunny day.

On that day we were taken from our ward after breakfast and check-ups, and were signed out for our excursion. We were to travel by car which meant that we could get a better view of the scenery than we usually did from an ambulance. I remember myself and Thomas being very giddy and high-spirited , I'm sure we stretched the patience of our 'tour guides' to the limit. My most vivid memory is that of the waterfall, the first I had ever seen. I am told that I actually stopped talking and looked in silence for a while at the cool, green water gushing down the dark and shady cliffside. I have returned recently to Glencar Waterfall and remembered every detail as if the twelve years in between had been just a blink. I'll tell you about the last visit in another chapter. My recollections of the remainder of the day include the bumpy roads of Leitrim and a visit to a castle, which had my imagination full of knights and dungeons for weeks.

We picnicked amongst breathtaking views of table mountains and the summer sun on the water. It was a far cry from dinner in the dayroom, looking through the window, with just a hill or two in the distance to tantalise us. Our al-fresco sandwiches tasted better than any hospital concoction and though they say that hunger is the best sauce, I think fresh air and freedom come a close second. Needless to say we slept well that night.

One day, after a series of examinations and muted discussions with assistants, Dr. Bell asked me if I'd like to go to Dublin. He thought it would be a good idea if I attended Our Lady's Hospital for Sick Children there, for further research and treatment.

Dublin! The big smoke, the capital city. The biggest town I had ever seen was Sligo and that only takes five minutes to drive through if the traffic's not bad. It was for my own good, and so my mother was informed by 'phone of the decision. She was understandably concerned; how, after all, would we keep contact over such distance? How long would I have to stay? She was assured that I would be well-looked after and we would be reunited soon.

Five hours in an ambulance for a sick traveller is no joke and though the journey was interesting, including two border crossings through Northern Ireland and some very nice scenery, my sick stomach didn't let me enjoy it and I prayed for the promised half-way break in Monaghan. There are two stages to travel sickness, the first is where you fear you're going to die, the second is when you fear you're going to live. I was well into the second by the time we reached Dublin and probably would have felt a lot worse if I'd known how many times in the future I was to make that hated journey. I remember an embarrassing situation on one of these journeys. It had been a sudden transfer to Dublin and I was not very well-prepared, being dressed as I was in just my pyjamas. This was fine until we reached Monaghan and stopped for our break. Well it was a decision between staying in a stuffy ambulance or going for tea and a snack, so in I marched to much turning of heads, I felt like I was on stage as I dined in my night wear and slippers. I knew how the famous must feel, being stared at all the time and ate as quickly as I could so as to reach my ambulance haven.

My first impression of Our Lady's, in Crumlin, was that it was big, very imposing and unfriendly. I suppose it's the same for anyone who goes somewhere where nobody knows them, you feel insecure and blame your surroundings. The feeling didn't last long after I found the television and surprise surprise, Thomas! He told me he had been sent there for treatment, however he wasn't his usual active self because he was confined to a wheelchair after surgery on his knees. Picture, if you will, two young lads on one wheelchair at high speed in a hospital corridor sounding like the chase scene from a lone ranger movie, and you will understand why the staff were a little annoyed at times. I was soon known to all the staff at Crumlin. We had a sneaking feeling that our days with the wheelchair were numbered!

One morning a sign was placed over my bed, 'Nil by mouth'. Translated for me this meant, 'No breakfast for Brendan'. I am fond of food and wasn't very pleased. A special test was to be done on me for which an empty stomach was vital; it didn't sound good. A tube was inserted through my mouth and down into my windpipe. I gagged, no wonder I was denied my toast. Two nurses held me whilst the procedure was accomplished, but I had to be sure not to cough while the tube was in place. An X-ray assured the team that it was correctly positioned and I was sent to bed. Another doctor came along with something that looked like an ordinary syringe. This he inserted into the tube and extracted fluid from my left lung where an abscess had formed. Further X-rays were taken after which the tube was removed. I feel sure the whole procedure was designed by Torquemada to elicit confessions from the unwilling. I was delighted to have the power of speech restored and had numerous questions to ask.

Thankfully, not all my time was taken up by examinations and there were plenty of hours for leisure, although I had to limit myself to what was 'in-house'. One evening when Thomas was busy, I found a jigsaw. Five hundred pieces of puzzle waiting to be assembled. It was a world map. I had to give it a try, and was soon absorbed in the task, compelled to see the finished product: countries and cities fitting together, little by little. Sometimes, to my dismay others would put a piece or two together, but I wanted to achieve the goal of completing a whole jigsaw myself. So a new pastime was discovered, one perfectly suited to me. The beauty of jigsaws is that the hands and eyes can work away without making ferocious demands on a limited oxygen supply.

So my stay in Dublin wasn't as bad as I expected, meeting Thomas meant that I wasn't too lonely and the staff were fantastic. When I was finally allowed home I was almost sad to leave. However, I had not seen my family for almost a month and couldn't bear to be away for much longer. Indeed, as the ambulance drove me the long miles home I wondered if they still remembered their second son.

Although it was delightful to be back home with the family, I was growing more aware of the appalling conditions in which they had to live, day in, day out. Compared to the relatively comfortable and hygienic environment of a hospital, our seventy-year-old cottage at Carn was like 'the Black Hole of Calcutta'. Moisture-laden walls played host to a flowerbed of fungus, the spores of which delighted in provoking my brothers' asthma attacks, and did me little good into the bargain. In place of the original wallpaper pattern we had unique designs in green mould, enhanced by the odd snail trail. I remember one occasion when my father picked up a drinking glass, only to find a pronged pair of snail's eyes looking at him over the rim! The local authority was considering our need for a move, but we were warned of the long queue of those awaiting new council houses.

4
—

BIRDS OF A FEATHER

Although I was never too good at concentrating on the educational study and exercises which Mother prescribed for me, a natural perversity made me quite willing to take over my two younger brothers' homework. Seamus and Kevin would often come home in despair, their long day of schoolwork not yet over. They envied, a wee bit, the fact that I was able to close the text books mid-afternoon and not have to open them again until the next morning. What I didn't have to do, of course, I wanted to do!

One little problem was that my hands were always extremely sweaty, leaving tell-tale dirty marks, and spreading ink stains all over the copy books. The teachers grew suspicious of how the two younger McLoughlin boys had become so uniquely messy in their work. Persistent questioning elicited the truth of what was going on backstage, so I had to abandon the practice.

My hands were not to be left idle though. I was introduced to light housework, and taught everything I would ever need to know about home management, from keeping the range ablaze to knowing when the next bill was due to land through the letterbox. At fourteen years of age I was much more aware of these essentials than my peers, who tended to think that clean clothes came from heaven, and money sprouted in the back garden. My mother had the wisdom to ensure that I would be well able to look after my own affairs in the days ahead, and that the unscrupulous could never make a fool of her disabled son.

It was a hard job trying to keep any semblance of order in our little old rat-infested cottage. Thankfully, the county council saw fit to commence work on building a new house for us just a few hundred yards away. We were happily encouraged by the progress of construction which was taking place within view of our front window. But it was all happening too slowly for Kevin, whose chronic asthma had become alarmingly severe.

Our local G.P., Dr. McKee, found it necessary to refer him to Dr. Bell's clinic in Letterkenny for assessment as his breathing difficulty had gone beyond reasonable control. For convenience his appointment was arranged to co-incide with my next outpatient visit. Dr. Bell decided that we both required admission to Sligo General, so this time I would have the company of my eight-year-old brother. Kevin had never stayed in hospital before, and was more than a little apprehensive about what lay ahead of him.

Indeed he did not settle in too well at first and had ideas of us both going home together on the next bus! Apart from not having the fare, I told Kevin it was unwise to leave a place where everyone had our best interests at heart. Although being a hospital patient was now very much part of my life, I still remember those moments of loathing my surroundings, especially my first few days in Crumlin, so I could empathise with how he felt. Fortunately the staff at Sligo General were like a second family to me, and made a great fuss in looking after my brother.

As Kevin was so young, hospital regulations required that he should be in his bed, counting sheep, at eight o'clock. He was none too impressed by this rule, being a television addict like myself. The very first evening, I took him to the dayroom to watch a late film. Like me, Kevin was small for his age, so I was able to hide him underneath the seat I occupied, away from the eyes of the nurses. There was one remaining problem in that Matron's schedule would often include an 11.00 p.m. round to ensure that the younger patients had counted all their sheep. The solution was simple enough. On my advice, Kevin sneaked back to his bed just long enough for Matron to come and go!

She was the strictest person we encountered. Unlike the other members of staff who ignored the by now inevitable high-speed trolley rides, she would shake her head and march us back to the wards. "Some people here," she would point out, "are sick!" I'm sure she must have been glad to see the back of us when we were discharged and sent back home to the arms of our welcoming family. For Kevin this was a once off 'holiday' in Sligo General, and his asthma was now under better control with the extra medication. There were still times when our mother would have to anxiously watch over the two of us as we struggled for breath during simultaneous attacks of gasping for air.

Whether or not some of the wheezing and coughing was precipitated by our bedtime activities remains open to question! When our mother had bid us sweet dreams we might sometimes get the urge to indulge in a pillow fight, resulting in a room filled with flying feathers. That is one thing we'd never have got away with in hospital. Like many cottagers in rural Ireland, we kept poultry in the back yard. For the fun of seeing more feathers flying when the chickens got drunk, I used to feed them spoonfulls of the Buckfast Wine which I was given to build me up. Worse still, I once got hold of a pellet gun and took a potshot at Mother's drake. Thankfully my aim was bad and only the ground beneath his rear end suffered the hit. But, there were other birds belonging to nobody which served as missile targets. A family of crows nested in the chimney pot and when the youngsters took flight we tried to stone them!

At this stage in my beligerent early teens I weighed a mere four- and-a-half stone, to the present day I have managed to gain just one-and-a-half more. Although my small frame accounts for some of the meagre impact on the scales, I have always been terribly lacking in flesh and muscle. The general illness caused most of my malnourishment, but the thing that turned out to be doing more harm than good was the twice weekly visits to Letterkenny for physiotherapy. The journeys made my stomach so sick that I couldn't keep anything down at all for up to a day after. When my mother pointed this out, Dr. Bell was in agreement that increased home physiotherapy was the best option.

It was thought wise to apply for a wheelchair now, as my general mobility was set to disimprove. We knew that the time would soon come when I would not be able to move far from the house under my own steam. As it was, my joints were prone to developing a build-up of fluid so I was instructed to perform frequent gentle exercise in order to prevent permanent confinement to the wheelchair. My parents bought me a child's bicycle, just the right size for an undergrown teenager, which provided a suitable means for exercising my legs. Also, my father, being good with his hands, constructed a special framework of exercise bars which helped to develop strength in my arms. All this limbering up activity, which took place out of doors where there was space and fresh air, attracted some rather unwelcome attention. A few local busybodies troubled themselves to report us to the authorities for receiving benefit we shouldn't be getting as I was 'obviously a fit and able child'. Needless to say, they were informed of their misinterpretation of the facts. They hadn't seen my medical reports nor did they see what was happening to me behind closed doors.

More and more of my time was spent away from the pillow fights, drunken chickens and unfortunate crows. Sligo General became such a regular venue that I could calculate with fair accuracy when my next 'holiday' was due. Between my precarious illness, her husband's unpredictable behaviour, and the many other hardships that were her burden to carry, Mother's own health began to deteriorate. The first signs of her ill health were obvious to me after I returned home from one of my 'vacations'. I was upset to find her looking very pale and drawn, and behaving in a slow, quiet manner that was not her own. Although she did her best to reassure me that she was now feeling quite alright, deep down I felt that she had suffered something more serious than a passing bout of 'flu. From this time onwards I was a bit more anxious with every parting.

5

—

JINGLE BELLS

Not unlike the experiences of many other families and individuals in difficult circumstances, we found Christmas to be the most stressful time of the year. I'm sure Santa Claus' first impression of Ireland is what he finds down the chimneypots of Donegal, it being the county nearest to his native North Pole. Here he would be introduced to our strange Gaelic tongue which although still very much outspoken by English, is most frequently to be heard in Donegal households. When Santa came down our chimney he must have heard some strange sounds indeed. Not Gaelic, but rather a slurred form of English emerging from my father's heavily intoxicated vocal cords. My mother has always said that she doesn't mind a 'drinking man' but she was hard put to tolerate the aggressive nature of my Dad when he got very drunk, and Yuletide was his zenith as far as the excuses for consuming alcohol went. All I can think is that there musn't have been a drop left for poor old Santa. What hospitality!

There were times that my father did show that he cared about his family. He built a swing for us in the garden, bought a child's bicycle, and constructed the exercise bars. He was brought up in poverty himself, he had an alcoholic father, and he never learned to read or write. Alcoholism is a terrible sickness, I would call it a western epidemic. When such a person is sober they can be as nice as anything, but when they drink something peculiar happens. I think Dr. Jekyll must have had a fair amount of alcohol in his potion because it had almost the same effect on my Dad. The nice side of him built those exercise bars, but the bad side of him beat up my mother. He was growing worse as the years went by.

Still, even if Mother hadn't got her husband's co-operation over the Christmas arrangements, she at least had mine. As I spent nearly all of my time at home with her I had plenty of opportunity to exercise my hands in putting up the decorations, writing cards, wrapping presents and preparing the pudding and mince pies. Each year we crossed our fingers that I would not be in hospital. I came close to that a few times, and Dr. Bell always tried to ensure that this would be avoided. I remember, when I was fourteen, being released from Sligo on the proviso that I return five days after Christmas for continuation of I.V. antibiotic therapy. On that occasion I was a very naughty boy and failed to fulfil my side of the bargain. Mother was torn between forcing the issue and upsetting me after having fared so well at home, or letting me have my way. I had my way, that time.

The very next year I was hospitalised with pleurisy very close on Christmas, and this time Dr. Bell proved that his memory was as long as his list of patients. He told me straight that he wasn't going to release me as he didn't trust me to return. I started feeling very sorry about last year's misdemeanor. The beds in my ward were becoming vacant one by one. Fewer mouths were left to converse with. There were still the remindful bits of tinsel and paper lanterns trying desperately hard to look 'in place' around the clinical decor. Then, there was the prospect of forfeiting the delights of my mother's home-cooked turkey for what I guessed would be the lesser delectation of a hospital bird. Of course, there would be no buses to bring any of my family to be with me on Christmas day. It all seemed too depressing to contemplate!

When Mother found me in this unhappy state she went at once to see Dr. Bell. Half an hour later she returned to my bed with the best

Christmas present imaginable – news that she had managed to bail me out. She had reassured him that she would undertake to see me put in an ambulance heading back to Sligo on New Year's Eve. Dr. Bell had warned her about the risks of my not continuing with the present treatment. There would be no softly softly approach if I did not comply, and who was I to argue!

January often brought snow to Donegal, when everywhere was white, and black, and enormously silent. Snow meant isolation to a young boy who could not risk catching cold building snowmen. I stayed indoors, but I wasn't bored. I had a large family to tease me and to make housework for me to do. We always said that Kevin left a trail of laundry everywhere he went, so if he got lost he'd be sure to find his way back. After Christmas there were always jigsaws to make. I would piece together a Nordic fjord scene or a pretty English cottage-garden picture, all the time wishing that someone would make a jigsaw of parts of Donegal. I mean, there I was, doing puzzles of places I have never seen in real life, and yet here I lived, surrounded by beautiful mountains and farmlands worthy of a place on any jigsaw box.

Although we didn't take a summer holiday, at least we could look forward to the odd day-trip to the seaside resort of Bundoran. This south Donegal town is reputed to have the longest street in Ireland, lined with hotels and amusement arcades. My brothers and I had worked out some devious ways of getting the gambling machines to part with a little of their takings. It was only a matter of a few pennies, the joy was in the sheer thrill of being daring, of getting the better of a machine. When we got tired of this we took ourselves down to the beach, to splash about at the edge of the enormous Atlantic breakers, and explore the quieter waters of the rock pools which abound with myriad wee fishes. Although we lived in the heart of Donegal, far away from our magnificent coast, there were no happier moments than those we spent by the sea.

My older brother Gerard, who is the quietest and most serious-minded member of our clan, would often accompany me on the very short walks I was able to manage. On one of these occasions we became fascinated by something that looked like tapioca floating on a pond. It was frogspawn, and as we examined further we discovered a host of maturing little frogs in their various stages of development. I slipped at the edge of the pool, cutting my foot on the edge of a sharp stone. Gerard immediately came to the rescue and started removing dirt from the wound. Then he saw what he thought was a tadpole in the cut and pulled at it. I yelled in agony – he was, in fact, pulling at a vein!

I was fifteen-years-old, full of spirit, but without the legs to carry me further than a few hundred metres down the hillside road, let alone back up again. I had almost grown resigned to my lack of mobility and was content that my life be centred around my immediate environs. To me, hospital provided the alternative scene, apart from the very occasional seaside trips. Mother had pressed hard to get a long-term loan of a wheelchair from the authorities so that at least I could be pushed the few miles down to Ballybofey town, and see people other than patients, nurses, doctors, physiotherapists and ambulance drivers. The wheelchair that was eventually given to us proved to be less than suited to the rough country 'boreens' which characterised our local road network. It was the small-wheeled type, fine for wheeling about indoors or on smooth city pavements, but hard put to cope with muck and potholes. Still, it was a step in the right direction, and we had to make do with it until such time as we could persuade the authorities to give us a more practicable model.

Another item that we really needed badly was a proper physiotherapy board. Mother had to 'play the drums' on my chest, sides and back a few times every day to loosen the mucus from my lungs, and for this to be effective I had to be lying at a slope with my head lower than my feet – the technical term being 'postural drainage'. In order to achieve this position on my ordinary bed we had to construct a slope with an arrangement of pillows, which was not entirely satisfactory. On the one hand we had the doctors emphasising the importance of proper physiotherapy, that it was my greatest weapon against infection and further lung damage, and on the other, we had to beg and wait and wait for the right equipment to carry it out in the recommended fashion.

Dr. Bell decided to send me to Dublin again, this time to an outpatients' clinic with a Dr. Taylor at the Harcourt Street Children's Hospital. The appointment was arranged for nine-thirty in the morning which meant that Mother and I would have to travel down the evening before and seek bed and breakfast for the night. We travelled down with local mini-bus driver, Joe Francie Marley, who was a great man to keep us entertained for the journey. It made a change from being transported by ambulance, but this time, instead of being able to stay in the hospital we were left outside, and we had to trek around the neighbourhood in search of accommodation. Mother had never been to Dublin before in her life, so it was a new and strange environment for her. It was six-thirty in the evening, and there seemed to be only expensive hotels, in the vicinity. Finally we came across a real bed and breakfast, like those that abound in Donegal, and they had a room for us. There were two single beds in the room, but as the night was perishing cold and the heating hadn't been turned on, we resorted to sharing one of them in the hope that our bodies would heat one another. We thought the Dubs must be a very hardy lot!

We got slightly lost trying to find our way back to Harcourt Street Hospital the next morning, but at least we managed to be in time for the appointment. After a physical examination which proved the left lung to be badly congested again, the doctor asked me to blow as hard as I could into a tube which would feed the breath through an instrument that showed the reading on a dial. A satisfactory reading would be two hundred, but I was only able to push the hand as far a ninety. Three more efforts proved no better and it was decided to detain me for 'a few days' for further tests. Mother had to leave me as she could not afford the expense of any further nights' accommodation.

I underwent a very rigorous and intensive series of tests, such as I had never experienced previously. These included an electrocardiograph (E.C.G.) and pulmonary stress tests, to evaluate how my heart and lungs were coping with various degrees of physical exertion. Sweat tests were repeated, this time with the aid of blow heaters and blankets to induce perspiration. An extraordinary number of blood analyses were done as well as what I was told were small tissue samples, taken from my side. Apparently the E.C.G. results did not please Dr. Taylor, and he ordered it to be repeated. He also performed a bronchoscopy in the operating theatre to have a look directly inside my lungs. A polyp was discovered growing into, and blocking, my nasal passages, not helping my breathing problem. I was sent across the city to St. James' Hospital, for half a day, to have it removed under local anaesthetic.

My 'couple of days' had turned into another three weeks of being totally separated from my family, so I returned home without fond memories of the capital city.

6
—

THE WILL TO SURVIVE

It took quite a few weeks for Harcourt Street Children's Hospital to send on their report about me to Dr. Bell. And when their findings came to his attention the news was not too good. He summoned Mother to have a serious talk with him, after which her obviously distressed state aroused my suspicion in no uncertain manner. I knew quite well that he'd given a very poor prognosis. I put the words into her mouth and she came clean. What she had been told was that it looked unlikely that I would live for more than six months. Apparently Dr. Bell himself was devastated, I had been one of his star patients and presented a real challenge to his professional capabilities. He had kept me alive against the odds thus far, and now it seemed that I was going to die no matter what treatment was given.

It was suggested to Mother that I might discontinue with the intravenous antibiotic treatment which necessitated regular three week hospital stays and instead opt for outpatient care and home treatment with antibiotics in tablet form. That sounded like the right idea to us if I had only six months to live. Why spend half of what precious life you have left in hospital when you can be with your family? Of course we understood that I could become gravely ill at some stage, and then require the professional, hospital, nursing-care that was beyond my mother's scope. But in the meantime I was going to live life to the fullest in terms of doing all the simple things that I enjoyed so much. A death sentence is hard to take on board fully, you carry on believing that you will survive.

There was one novelty to help take our eyes off the black cloud. Our new house was ready for us to move into. We were delighted to bid farewell to the slimy old cottage and take up residence in our spanking new little house, specially built for us by the council. Whatever chance I had of keeping reasonably well, was greatly helped by the new clean environment. And if we ever got lonely for our old home all we had to do was look out the window at it!

The old place had been my father's family home before my parents got married, and after we abandoned it his sister continued living there. A few months later Dad took up his belongings and went to live with her. I think that some of his problems centred on jealousy over the attention that I was getting. Instead of co-operating with Mother and earning her respect he acted like a beligerant child, creating havoc during his drunken bouts. We thought that at least now we might have some peace, but being on the outside he made sure that his intrusions to our household were often none too polite. One thing I must point out is that he got on well with my sisters, and they quite missed their Dad. Indeed we all wished that it didn't have to be like this, that he could have had more self-respect.

Mother's health problem was clearly manifesting itself now, with all the stress and strain. She was suffering from angina, a heart condition that caused her to develop severe chest pains when she pushed herself too hard. These attacks were extremely worrying, and she was told by the doctor to take it very easy. This was a difficult instruction to obey under the circumstances. I was constantly worried that she might have a major heart attack with unthinkable consequences.

A curious thing, or maybe not – a close relative of hers died prematurely around this time of what was supposed to be 'Farmer's Lung'. Most likely, being a rural woman, that was the cause of her death, but looking back now we wonder if she suffered from the familial disease that I have.

Shortly after my dreadful prognosis, Mother and I made a day pilgrimage to the Marian Shrine at Knock, Co. Mayo. The 'Lourdes of Ireland', as some people call it, has become almost as internationally famous in recent years, thanks to the efforts of the equally famous local priest, Monsignor Horan. He was a great activist (a term once applied to me in later years by Fr. Michael Cleary on his radio show) and a very ambitious man who set out to put Knock on the map. Some people thought he was daft when he planned to have a major airport constructed in this desolate, sparsely populated, western part of Ireland but he lived to see his dream come true. The Monsignor made his last living journey to Lourdes, where he died suddenly, after departing by jet from 'Horan International Airport'.

This was our second visit to Knock, before the days of seeing jets bringing down the faithful from the skies. We were looking for a miracle, no less. In whatever form or shape it should manifest, we were praying hard that something might happen to prevent me from dying. Ever since Our Lady appeared to three local villagers in the eighteenth century, many cures have been reported among the sick who have devoted a day of prayer here in Her honour. We stood inside the glass encasement which surrounds the outside of the old church wall where the vision took place. The 'glasshouse' was crammed with pilgrims, queues outside waited for us to move on to the many other holy venues of Knock. The interior of the old church is a chapel devoted to the Exposition of The Blessed Sacrament, where people pray before Christ's Body. We did the Stations of The Cross before entering the modern octagonal Basilica, where we attended Mass during which I received the Blessing of the Sick.

Before departing on the bus for home, which was over a hundred miles away, we gathered an array of religious souvenirs to keep as reminders of our pilgrimage, and which would inspire us to keep praying, to keep fighting my battle to survive. We came home armed with bottles of holy water, medals, statues and pictures. At least the holy water is free of charge, but the local tradespeople run a thriving business selling statue-shaped containers to put it in!

In desperation my mother began writing letters to priests, and anyone whom she thought might have great impact with the 'Man Above'. From priests she went on to bishops. It didn't stop there either. She went right to the top of the Roman Catholic hierarchy. A letter was put in the box down at our local post office, addressed to the Pope. We have a collection of sympathetic replies with pledges of prayers, including one from His Holiness, Pope John Paul II.

I was presently taking antibiotics by mouth, continuing with my mother's physiotherapy, my medical regime being supported with visits from our then local G.P., Dr. McKee. I was also attending the outpatients clinic in Letterkenny, but successfully avoiding admissions. Being a special patient to him, Dr. Bell had kept me under his care, longer than he normally would as a child-care specialist. So the time came when I was handed over to Dr. Bannon, an adult-care physician at the same hospital. He supported the home treatment schedule.

As my health deteriorated Mother sought the advice from a local woman who was known to have knowledge of old country cures. She knew these would do no harm, and might indeed help me. The recipe she was given for my complaint required the purchase of half-a-pound of brown onions, a pound of brown sugar and half a bottle of whiskey. This concoction had to be blended together and buried underground for six weeks. My mother prepared and bottled the mixture, while my father, who believed in the old country methods, played his part in putting it securely underground. In the meantime I used steam inhalations to help combat the increasing congestion on my chest. My poor appetite allowed me to eat little, and my diet was supplemented with vitamins and minerals, including halibut oil capsules. I went through a very severe time of coughing and feverishness whilst the potion was 'maturing', or whatever it was doing underground. In fact I felt as though I might soon be joining it!

On the appointed date the bottle was dug up from the soil, surprising us all by the clarity of its contents. It smelt quite piquant and attractive to me. It even tasted nice, though some of my family thought it was awful. I wouldn't have cared what it was like anyway so long as it offered me a chance of feeling better. A few spoonfuls two or three times a day, the old woman recommended. Right enough, my worst symptoms had greatly diminished within a week of taking this remedy. None of us understood how or why it worked. It's hard to put it down to auto-suggestion, the 'placebo effect', when you're dealing with a very serious condition such as mine. There is probably some scientific explanation, but as I'm not a scientist I can't establish the reason. To this day, when at home, I still take a potion which is based on this recipe, but with the inclusion of garlic.

The six months I was given to live came and went, and almost a year later here I was, still in the land of the living. There were no flies hanging about me, the vultures seemed to have taken wing and gone back to their eyries. I still knew that new young birdies could always hatch sometime, however, this prolonged trauma in my life inspired my *Will To Survive*.

7
—

YOUNG AND NOT SO CAREFREE

Six months didn't mean much, as they say, 'you know neither the day nor the hour', so it couldn't really be a worry to me. I had already outlived my sell-by date so life was a bonus I appreciated and enjoyed, until...

Another admission to Letterkenny General. "Pneumonia" said the doctors, "very serious". Under Dr. Bannon I was being treated for immotile cillia syndrome. This was a new diagnosis to me and did not involve the use of the enzymes (Cotazym-b), which I had been taking for some years previously. This is used to help cystic fibrosis patients digest their food and at that time I was not considered to be a C.F. patient.

I feel that this is a very important part of my medical history. I was no longer being treated for the disease I had because the doctors weren't sure just what it was. We sufferers of cystic fibrosis cannot fully absorb the nutrition from our food without supplementary enzymes. I was taken off them at seventeen years of age and put back on at twenty-four years, when C.F. was finally verified. It's a mystery I survived the intervening years and no surprise that I suffered continuous indigestion and never gained any weight.

Well I recovered from the pneumonia and was soon back to 'normal' and trying to enjoy myself. For this I needed to be roadworthy, I still had my old wheelchair but it was the small-wheeled variety and not a serious option on Irish roads and paths. The health service obliged with a large-wheeled one and my social activities got a much needed boost. Brendan could hit the town in style, or could he?

Saturday evenings in our house were pretty typical. People screaming for hairbrushes and waiting to get into the bathroom, sporadic arguments, spraying of hair and armpits and anything that moved. Aftershave and pop music and singing in front of the mirror. There I'd be, getting ready for Jackson's Disco in Ballybofey town centre wondering what nice young ladies I might encounter that night.

One particular Saturday, clean-shirted and washed, I set off to a disco in nearby Killygordon, normal as anyone if you could ignore the wheelchair and my Mother who had to accompany me lest I collapse (most of the really good nights I did collapse!). My uncle drove us to the disco hall whereupon we tried to gain entry, three pounds fee clutched in hand. "No, he's too young", exclaimed the girl in the ticket office. We smiled and explained that my disease had prevented me growing but she still refused. My uncle swore, my mother swore – I was nearly twenty after all! We told her to ring the Ballybofey police who knew me, we told her to phone my doctor who would verify. Still I was refused entry, I think if the Pope himself had insisted I was old enough she would have stuck to her guns. I half admired her stubbornness, but thought she might have had other motives; perhaps only the able-bodied are suitable for discos. We 'thanked' her profusely and left. Waste of time washing my hair.

So I decided it was to be Jackson's from now on, and two nights a week at that! Mother was anxious that I develop as normally as possible and try all that my peers did, so I stepped out on Fridays and Saturdays. Friday was ladies night, so I was sure to meet someone. However, most of the population of Ballybofey had the same idea so the place got very hot and crowded. I remember one night I overdid it a little, I strongly suspect that someone put vodka in my mineral water. I was convinced I could dance the pants off Michael Jackson and I hit the dance floor. A few minutes later I hit it again, literally. I was carried off by my friends and deposited in chair until I was collected. I vomited all night and vowed 'never again' until the next time.

Occasionally I was badly treated at a disco, insulted about my stature, told I was just using a wheelchair to get welfare allowance and numerous other sillinesses. I didn't pay much heed, I knew it was the accusers who were showing themselves up. Going home, however, it could get a little annoying. Mother would have to push my chair up the winding paths to my home and sometimes people we knew would stop as if to give us a lift and speed off as we reached the car. Once someone offered to push the wheelchair for us and let me and it roll down a hill damaging the wheelchair, but fortunately not me, in the process.

My father was living only a few yards from us at this time. Being so close meant that whether we liked it or not we heard a lot from him. On many occasions he was abusive and violent, causing Mother greater stress than she was able for. He would always be drunk on these occasions; when he wasn't, he was a fine man to talk to. But gradually the alcoholic took over. Mother wrote an endless stream of letters to anyone she thought could help and eventually ended up in court fighting for a barring order which would prevent my father from having contact with us. She won and things changed a lot for the Mc Loughlin family. Alcohol had taken my father, now the courts took the alcoholic.

The strain had been severe and my Mother had a mild heart attack. The doctor advised lots of rest. Her heart condition was associated with high blood pressure, and not alone that but she had a peptic ulcer to contend with. Clearly she had to relax; a life spent caring for a sick family with an alcoholic to make things unbearable had taken its toll. From now on she would have to hire a taxi to get me into town for the disco, instead of risking her life pushing me up the steep hill. This, of course, we could only afford to do one night per week. We all vowed that she would do less in the future.

I felt we deserved a little good news after all this and I wasn't to be disappointed. We heard that a house we had enquired about was available for rent. It was located in the townland of Knock in Ballybofey (not to be confused with the Knock in county Mayo where The Blessed Virgin is said to have appeared). It was rented to us by Mr. Horace White who was going to live in Northern Ireland until he got married. It suited us just fine. The rent wasn't too high, it was nearer to the town and as it was further from my father, it would make life a lot more relaxing for my mother. We moved as soon as was possible and got used to another new home.

I decided at this time that we needed a break and insisted on a little holiday to Bundoran. It would be a new experience for us, having been impossible before, because of Dad. We caught a bus to the seaside and rented a caravan from some nice locals who very kindly threw an extra few nights in for free. We had a fantastic time. Plenty of air, sun, laughter, rest and recuperation, just what the doctor ordered!

Money was as tight as ever in those days, however. The allowances I received were used in part to pay rent and no one in the house was employed. The assistance I received from the Cystic Fibrosis Association had to be stopped as at that time I was not diagnosed as having C.F. But we managed and indeed we were happy. I planned and dreamed like any young man. I fancied myself at the wheel of a car and thought of ways of achieving this financially. I dreamt of going to

Lourdes some day, but even that, though less expensive than a car, was beyond our means. I made enquiries and took tentative steps towards fulfiling these dreams in spite of knowing how unlikely I was to succeed. Anyhow, whether my dreams came true or not, I knew I'd enjoy the fun and family atmosphere of holidays in Bundoran. Family, love, yet more freedom from hospital stays for nearly eighteen months, and good times, what more could I ask for?

8
—

TAKING HEART

Mother was worried, she had noticed a deterioration in my health. There didn't seem to be a week where I wasn't fighting some infection or other. She would swear that pharmaceutical companies would close for sure if it wasn't for our custom. The journey to Letterkenny Hospital was becoming as routine as swallowing my medicine and Dr. Bannon seemed to frown more as he gazed at X-rays of darkening lungs. Mother had read somewhere about the British-based surgeon, Madgi Yacoub's pioneering work in heart and lung transplant surgery, and she wanted to know more. Her initial enquiry invoked such a spasm of laughter from one of my doctors that she thought she must have missed her vocation on the Irish comedy stage. But like a good comedian, she didn't laugh at her own joke, and the medical man who was her audience thought a little more on her words.

One bout of infection lead to my being rushed to Letterkenny for emergency treatment. The thermometer was staying stubbornly in the hundreds, I had cramps in my bowels and wasn't responding to antibiotics. A fan was placed by my bed to stop me frying and to tell you the truth I was worried. What if the temperature didn't come down soon? Convulsions? Brain damage? I was delighted when I was treated with strong intravenous antibiotics which at last had some effect. I could let myself think a little further ahead than the next few hours.

To say that my illness at this stage was confusing is an understatement. Looking back on it now I can see that for many years I didn't actually know what was wrong with me. Medical documents trace a varied list of names I believed were my actual illness. The first was good old immotile cillia syndrome. That, as the name suggests, tells me that the cillia or little hairs lining the lung tissue were not moving. Therefore they were not doing their job of brushing mucus and foreign bodies (dust, etc) from my lungs. So it all builds up and leads to the next big word on the lips of my doctors: bronchiectasis. This describes the condition of the tubes in my lungs after years of fighting against the odds to supply me with air. They had become scarred, and distorted, prone to developing abscesses. Bad news, and all the more so because it is only a part of my entire disease, and not the fundamental defect. I was not aware of the reason for the condition.

Meanwhile there I was, tied to my bed by drips in Letterkenny with the good doctors worrying over the state I was in. It was decided by Dr. Bannon that I should be sent to Dublin to be seen by a friend of his, a respiratory consultant named Dr. Conor Burke, at the James Connolly Memorial Hospital. It would be in his hands to decide whether or not I might be a suitable candidate for a transplant, and to make the necessary arrangements for all the stages leading up to it.

The hospital is in a village called Blanchardstown on the outskirts of Dublin. I was used to seeing a townscape from my other hospital windows, here I saw countryside and farm animals, a pleasant change. Inside, the hospital was much the same as any other, except that here I was bedded in one of the many single rooms available. This ensured that as a frequent stay patient I would be afforded as much privacy as well as sociability that I liked to enjoy. It meant that I could have more freedom to 'entertain' visitors and fellow patients without disturbing anyone else. I was told that they would have to carry out their own series of tests including pulmonary function tests, blood gases, and all the usual tests involving provision of samples. A week of tests later and I was sent home again.

After two subsequent visits to Blanchardstown my mother and I were summoned to meet with several specialists including one from America, one from London and Dr. Burke himself. They all had a look and told us that the test results were not good My lower left lung which was not working at all, served only as a breeding ground for infection, and may have to be removed. As things turned out, I was spared having to undergo this particular operation. I was suffering from immotile cillia syndrome, my lungs were about ready for the dustbin anyway!

It didn't take a genius to figure out what they were saying, "Mc Loughlin, you're in rag order!" They were giving it to me straight, I mean at that stage I was twenty-two years old, weighing about six stone and gasping from one infection to the next, I knew I was sick and after all the years in hospital I was aware that the treatments were palliatives, very far from cures. I was used to living with that, for a healthy person it may have been bad news but to me it was as obvious as telling a man with one leg that he only needed one stocking!... Next 'problem' please. While you're alive there is hope and you can keep ahead of the negative prognosis .

About a year after my meeting with the experts, I was given some good news by Dr. Burke in Blanchardstown, there was a possibility that the quality of my life could be vastly improved by a heart and lung transplant This was exactly what Mother and I had asked about, and thought about; that I would be considered for the recently pioneered surgery that gave hope of a near normal life to those who had resigned themselves to a lingering death. There was also another angle to the story, I could possibly be the first such transplant to be carried out in

Ireland. If it came about, the operation would be performed in Dublin's Mater Hospital by the country's only heart transplant surgeons, Maurice Neligan and Freddie Woods. I was admitted to this city centre hospital for five days to be assessed for the surgery.

Two months later a special appointment was made for my mother and I to have a lengthy talk with members of the transplant team in the Mater. The two surgeons involved had carried out quite a number of successful heart transplants over the past couple of years, and were now aspiring to set up a new heart and lung transplant programme in Ireland. Until the government consent to this, all transplant patients are sent to one of the British centres. At this point it looked as though the Irish programme would be instituted in the not too distant future. All I knew was that I would consent to be done anywhere that would do me quickest, although Mother had followed up so many encouraging stories about Madgi Yacoub that she would then have been happiest to see me directly in his hands! In any case this visit to the Mater was an educational exercise in introducing us to the reality of what it might be like 'on the night'. The considerable risks were again explained, and we were brought psychologically through the stages from awakening after the major surgery, through recovery, and to the involved aftercare that would continue for the rest of my life. We were introduced to the intensive care unit, to all the machinery and tubes that would be protruding from my near-naked body for the initial period of my recovery. Mother had to picture the scenario of her first visits to me, dressed up as she would have to be in surgical attire, mask and all, to prevent cross infection.

If and when donor organs became available I would be contacted by phone or the police immediately, an escort would take me by the fastest transport to the Mater if the operation were to be performed there or to the airport, if in Britain. I would be prepared on the way and arrive drugged and almost ready for anaesthetic. The operation would last eight hours and I would, with a bit of luck, regain consciousness soon after. Once in place the new heart is 'kick started' and the lungs are helped for a while by an artificial ventilation machine. Most people think it strange that the heart, if healthy, should also be transplanted, but technically, I was told, it is much simpler to do both as there are basically fewer bits to sew together! Moreover, the new heart has been friends with the new lungs for years, so they come to the recipient as a working team. Up to a week, maybe, in intensive care and then a further six to eight weeks in observation. After that there would be a strict anti-rejection regime implemented, during which time infections were to be avoided at all costs. The worst thing that could go wrong at that stage would be rejection. Every care is taken to ensure that the organs chosen are as close a match to the recipient as possible in relation to size and blood grouping, but nevertheless the new organs are a foreign body to the immune system and so must be destroyed. The immune system is therefore suppressed by drugs which are taken for the rest of the recipient's life. I was aware that I would still have to be a life-long frequenter of hospitals, there'd be no getting away from that.

There was a lot to think about, there were great risks involved, it would have to be the last resort. Nevertheless, it would have to be done before I became gravely ill, as my chances of surviving the surgery would then be minimal. I would receive lungs and heart from a young person who had been healthy and so must have died suddenly. I knew that those who consented to the use of their loved ones' organs always reported a feeling that at least some worth had come from a terrible tragedy. Someone is given a chance of life because of another's death. I knew that there was always a shortage of donors and that many die on waiting lists, despite the fact that the most critical cases are done first. Over the years a positive attitude has become a habit. Looking for the 'silver lining' is as routine as putting on my socks, it was the same here. I looked upon the transplant as the only way forward. I want to live with a respectable quality of life, I've been offered a chance and it would be wrong not to go for it. Otherwise I would probably whittle away what time I had gasping for each lungful. I enjoy life and plan to take every opportunity to continue doing so.

May was approaching and with it the prospect of my twenty-third birthday. Thanks to the dedication of the doctors who treated me, I could look forward to this with some degree of enthusiasm. We began saving for a holiday to our favourite Donegal seaside mecca, Bundoran. Even though we could barely afford it, we looked on our break as a necessity, not a luxury. Meanwhile I was doing my best to enjoy myself, and distract my mind from becoming too overstretched with worries about things over which I had no control. This was the great summer of 1990, memories of which will be cherished in the heart and soul of Irishmen (and women!) for years to come. Jack Charlton, manager of the Irish soccer team, had led his 'Army' into the quarter finals of the U.E.F.A. World Cup. I enthusiastically followed every single one of the matches on the television, and my notoriously loud voice must have been heard cheering by the lads in Italy! One of my prize possessions is a signed photograph of goalkeeper, Packie Bonner, a Donegal man himself. Between matches I made sure to enjoy regular visits to the disco and a few hangovers before my next sojourn to Dublin.

9
—

AN ILL WIND

The 19th of August 1990 is a day neither my family nor our good neighbours will ever erase from our memories. Only a week had elapsed since our return from Bundoran. Still full of talk about the summer holiday, we would often engage in such conversation with the various members of the McGowan family next door. Teresa McGowan, the mother, spoke to my own mother of the latest pursuits of her own children, and her hopes for their future. Most of her daughters and her only son were in or around their twenties and still living 'in the nest'. So the house next door was invariably a hive of activity with the comings and goings of cars, as each family member followed their own busy schedule.

My older brother, Gerard, would nearly always be found at Jackson's Disco of a Saturday night, and the 18th proved no different in this respect. On this particular night I stayed at home and went to bed quite early. At six o'clock in the morning I heard Gerard coming in. I thought it was odd that he should have stayed out so late as he wasn't much in the habit of doing this. Then I heard him waking up the household, knocking on bedroom doors, sobbing quietly in distress. Something very serious was wrong.

It didn't take long, a mere few seconds, for him to tell us what had happened. Actually believing it took minutes, maybe hours. I don't know how long it must have taken the McGowans to realise that their twenty-one-year-old son, Henry, was dead. The shocking news had reached the night owls of Ballybofey first, among them my brother who was the best of pals with Henry. The tragic accident happened when Henry was driving home alone from a night stint as D.J. for Donegal Highland Radio in Letterkenny. The spot where it happened is notorious for nocturnal fatalities, though it appears deceptively safe by day. In one fell swoop, without hint of warning, without time for words, a young life had ended. There seemed to be no purpose in it.

We immediately went into the McGowan household to try and share their unspeakable grief, and to help in any practical way that we could. Throughout the day more and more relatives and friends arrived from various parts of the country to stay with the bereaved family during the wake. Mother busily employed herself making cups of tea and sandwiches for everyone. By late evening time the house was full of people, most of them strangers to me, so I was invited to join some of the immediate family in a smaller room. In a situation like this it is impossible to know what to say, certainly no words can alter the shattering reality. One of the girls, Pauline, called me over to meet a family friend from Dublin who was about the same age as myself.

The young Dublin man was naturally as speechless as myself. I ventured to break the numbing silence by talking about my forthcoming operation. Poor Pauline tried to put on a brave face and give the impression that my conversation was of interest to her, but only a few minutes passed when she was required to console her weeping mother. I found myself still talking, trying to overcome my own tears. The quiet young man remained in his seat, listening attentively to what I had to say. He asked questions, not so much to probe or satisfy a morbid curiosity, but rather in a manner which conveyed sincere interest and empathy.

I had every wish to stay in the McGowan household through the night, but Teresa and her husband Patsy insisted that I go home to my bed and get some rest. Needless to say I found it impossible to get much sleep. Visions of Henry waving across from the garden, stepping into his car and driving off, or the echoes of his cheery voice coming across the airwaves of donegal Highland Radio filled my thoughts. It was difficult to believe that he would be laid to rest in a few hours time.

The funeral took place at the remote Seas i gCoineal Church and adjoining Cemetary, not far from where we lived. A large crowd attended, among the folks gathered there was the man I had spoken to during the wake. He was some distance away but gave a brief smile and a wave. We hadn't exchanged names.

A couple of weeks later I received a letter bearing a Dublin postmark. I opened it with some puzzlement as I didn't recognise the writing or signature of a 'Martin Byrne'. As I read through it, I discovered it was from the man at Henry's wake. In his letter he asked me when I was due for my next admission to Blanchardstown Hospital, and whether or not I would like him to visit me there. Of course I was delighted to encourage a new visitor, but little did I know at this stage that Martin Byrne was to play a major role in giving me the hope and courage that I was going to need so badly as my health began to reach its steepest decline.

True to his word, Martin showed up during my next episode at the Dublin hospital, and during subsequent stays. He never really spoke much about himself, instead preferring to be a good listener. However, I learned that he was working in Dublin Public Libraries and seemed to have a quite a broad range of interests. His main involvement was with youth drama, and it was through this that he had come to know the

McGowan family. During the summer of 1990 the European Youth Theatre Encounter was hosted by the city of Bonn in Germany, and both he and Kathleen McGowan were among the small Irish contingent there. He consequently became an occasional visitor to Ballybofey where 'Butt Drama Circle', of which Kathleen is a member, stage regular productions in the local theatre.

During the autumn we had a telephone installed at home, so that I could be contacted directly in the event of donor organs becoming available. This was a great advantage for when I was in hospital as it allowed more frequent communication between myself and the family. Prior to this my mother relied on the kindness of the McGowan family in letting her use their telephone. And it was also reassuring to know that medical or any other emergency help could be sought from the hallway of our own home, whatever the hour, day or night. The only trouble was that I soon got into the habit of calling home from Dublin every day I was hospitalised, only to find that the glutton of a public payphone was feeding hard and fast on my limited supply of pocket money!

Back home in Donegal, between routine admissions to Blanchardstown for reassessment, the winter months were cold and harsh. I didn't get out of the house much, not even to the Friday night local dance. My condition had deteriorated to such a degree that a lot of the time I was only able to walk from the bedroom to the kitchen or bathroom. At night I often had to use oxygen, and I dared not to lie prone. I had to sleep in a half sitting-up position or else I would almost drown in my own lung fluid.

My younger brother, Kevin, was on a 'CERT' cookery course in Bundoran, aspiring to be a fully-qualified chef. I missed him a lot, not alone for his dreadful untidyness, but for the late night company he provided whilst we viewed video or television films together. Seamus, younger still, was now working in Dublin which at least meant I had another visitor in Blanchardstown. School kept Martina away from the house during the day, and both Frances and Gerard were employed locally, but still, at least, sleeping and eating in the house! All of which meant that the housekeeping was shared between Mother and myself, though I could only handle the lightest of jobs on my 'good' days. Mother always insisted that her other children's social life and resultant future prospects would not be hindered by my circumstances. What was now bothering us about my sisters was the fact that they both had the tendency to develop very nasty chest infections. I certainly did not want to be a witness to any others like myself.

It was considered essential that I have the influenza vaccine in case an outbreak should occur during the winter months. I'm not sure which might have been the lesser of two evils, the illness itself or my idiosyncratic reaction to the immunisation. Within a few hours of receiving the jab I developed nausea and a fever. We took no notice of it until two days later when I became acutely ill. Mother called our local G.P., Dr. Mitchell in, and he had me carted off in the 'meat wagon' to Letterkenny Hospital where I spent the next eleven days with what very much felt like a bad dose of the 'flu!

Christmas time was always a worry to us as we well knew that my father would be extra indulgent with alcohol. Every day he passed by our house on the way in and out from the town. If Mother was alone in the house he could be in on top of her before she knew it, as her eyesight was very poor. This season I was entirely housebound so at least I could keep alert as to who was approaching the house and dive for the phone if necessary. Father was still under a Barring Order, and as things turned out he didn't risk a prison sentence. For this reason, and for the convenience it would provide, a town house was highly desirable. Shortly after our summer holiday we heard word that the county council had allocated houses in the town centre when we were away. This was a great disappointment as we had been ensured that they would be on offer on our return.

In spite of having a rather miserable Christmas being confined to the home and consuming high protein drinks instead of turkey, I was fortunate enough to get out to the New Year's Eve dance in Jackson's Hotel. A combination of a mild spell in the weather and the kindness of some local friends who took it upon themselves to transport and look after me, allowed me to have a most enjoyable night. For once in a very long time my mind took a break from thinking about the major operation ahead!

Once 1991 had got underway I thought it about time that I did something about making a public donor appeal. It was becoming all too obvious that I hadn't got unlimited time to play around with, and rather than sit around and wait for things to happen I realised there was something I could do for myself. During the autumn I had read about the death of a man who was awaiting a heart and lung transplant. In last minute desperation his family made a brave appeal through the media, but no donor organs became available. I was well aware that publicity would by no means guarantee a new set of parts for my body, but at least somebody else might benefit. These days it is important to make people aware that major transplant operations are no longer 'experimental'; they are a very worthwhile resort to try and effect a permanent cure for a variety of otherwise terminal illnesses.

I decided to contact our local radio station, Donegal Highland Radio, where my tragically deceased neighbour, Henry McGowan had worked. This station is renowned for being the most professionally run, local, broadcasting unit in Ireland, and has a very good following in the North-West. Their charming researcher, Maureen Gibbons – who left the national RTE broadcasting service to join Highland – secured an interview for me with presenter, Sean Doherty. I was given a date for an early morning slot, and prayed that I would be well enough to fulfil the appointment. On the morning in question I had to get up very early so as to cough away the night's accumulation of fluid. Impressive as it might sound, I had in mind to get more than a word in edgeways between the coughs and wheezes.

One of the main questions put to me centred on my fears about getting through the operation. My answer was that when you are facing a sure death sentence without it, then you fear less the operation itself. What I didn't express over the airwaves was my slight terror of being on radio for the first time! The family at home taped the interview for me, and as I discovered, there is nothing worse than hearing your own voice being played back. I could hear a very pronounced Donegal accent in every word I spoke. However, there was no doubt that I had got across, very well indeed what I wanted to say. One of the regional newspapers, *The Donegal Democrat*, covered my story on the same morning, and this bit of dual coverage whetted my appetite for nationwide publicity.

When I returned to Blanchardstown Hospital for my next little 'holiday', Martin discussed the possibilities of obtaining an interview on one of the RTE radio or even television programmes. We both realised that it is much easier to arrange something if you know people of import in that semi-state organisation, and neither of us did. So, both of us began by writing letters to the producers of a couple of the better-known programmes. The most that came of it was the appearance and disappearance of a researcher from a certain morning radio show.

One morning, in frustration, I penned a note to *The Sunday World* tabloid, knowing that many folks around Ireland spend the Sabbath glossing through its pages of easily-digested gossip. Previous donor appeals had appeared in this paper, and I was correct in believing that they would not ignore me. On the 14th April 1991, my mugshot and accompanying tale of woe appeared on one of its inside pages. At last I could wallow in the knowledge that people from all over the country would read of my existence.

That Sunday morning I phoned Martin from my home, and he raided the Dublin newsagents, obtaining copies to pass around his associates. Apparently the very next day, a colleague from the Dublin Libraries phoned him at the branch where he was working, partly on business and partly in response to *The Sunday World* article. She had followed other donor appeal stories and was curious to know what other publicity was in the offing. Martin told her that there was nothing definite afoot, and knowing her likely enthusiastic response to a challenge, he asked her if she could come up with any ideas. I wonder how Martin felt when he gave free rein to Martine Brangan because I have come to know the girl as a Rottweiler when it comes to getting her teeth into anything!

A Very Important Person must have been reading *The Sunday World* with her morning breakfast, for I received a well-wishing letter from Mary Robinson, the first lady President of Ireland, no less. This elite epistle, fittingly framed, has pride of place on the mantelpiece of our living room.

10

A GLOW OF LIMELIGHT

At this stage in my media campaign I had two Dublin friends who were acting on my behalf. The solidarity of two associates making personal appearances on journalistic doorsteps was to prove most successful in creating a nationwide appeal for a terminally ill man from Donegal. Martin Byrne and Martine Brangan's first conquest was in persuading the renowned broadcasting priest, Fr. Michael Cleary, to devote one of his *Dublin Tonight* radio shows on the subject of 'Brendan McLoughlin, the young man from Donegal awaiting a heart and lung transplant'.

This five-nightly programme is broadcast on 'Classic Hits, 98FM', a very popular independent radio station which can be received around much of Ireland, but alas, not Donegal. I was requested to phone in on the show during the late evening on Friday 28th April, though I was deaf to what Martin and Martine had been saying about me to Fr. Cleary and all the world, on the air. At least I knew Martine couldn't have said much because she had never met or spoken to me before this. Fr. Cleary was a good man to have at the helm as he had no vested interest in trying to 'catch you out' or stir up sensationalism for the sake of making an interesting programme. If there were any gaps in the conversation he would fill them in right away, without fuss.

Listeners were invited to phone in with relevant comments, anecdotes or suggestions. A fair number of calls were made to the programme, among them relatives of successful heart and lung and other transplant recipients. A couple of children spoke of the fact that they carry multi-donor cards, with all the options ticked, endorsed by their parents. Although the emphasis was never laid on financial need, two hoteliers made offers of weekend breaks, the proceeds of which were to go towards any expenses incurred by my mother's stay in England or Dublin, during my transplant period. One of the hoteliers was Brian McEniff, more famed as manager of the Donegal football team, than as owner of the Holyrood Hotel in Bundoran. For some reason no raffles were organised, nothing came of this.

One week following, Fr. Cleary had on his show, *Eyebank Ireland*, the organisation that harvests corneas for eye transplants, and once again the listeners were reminded of my story. Indeed it was interesting to see how many more related articles appeared here and there in the wake of my publicity. A couple of months later it was reported that there had been a dire shortage of organ donors in the first half of the year, but that 'this situation had changed as a result of recent appeals'.

The next weekend both Martin and Martine came up to my home in Ballybofey laden with folders, a picture camera and a video camera. I was beginning to gain expertise at being interviewed so it was no problem to 'perform', answering every question under the sun whilst Martin pointed his camcord lens pointing conspicuously in my direction. For the first time I met Martine in the flesh, and she seemed to have a real sense of purpose behind her slightly flirtatious and humorous facade. The information gathered, the photos and video shots were all going to be used for compiling a press release and portfolio for circulation among the media bodies.

My friends stayed for just a couple of hours after which they travelled further north to Letterkenny which they were using as a base for their Donegal campaign. A reporter and photographer from *The*

Derry People and Donegal News was sent to my house, and an extensive article was published in the journal a few days later which featured a picture of myself with my Mother and sister, Martina. A shorter story appeared in *The Donegal Democrat* under the very appropriate heading: 'BRENDAN'S PLIGHT TAKEN TO HEART BY DUBLIN FRIENDS'. The Letterkenny Cathedral parish newsletter gave me a mention which ensured I would be included in a few more prayers!

My Dublin friends also did two more radio interviews which didn't involve me directly. One was again with my pals on Donegal Highland Radio, and the second was fitted in en route back to Dublin with North-West Radio in Ballyshannon, south Donegal. Throughout, it was stressed that my condition was deteriorating at a frightening pace. I later learned that Martin had confided to Martine that he had seen a big change since the day we had first met, and that was only seven months earlier. My downhill progression had not been so obvious to him looking at me resting quietly on a hospital bed as it was when he compared the only two occasions he knew me to be out of pyjamas.

Among the things they troubled themselves with was putting in a little word to the local politicians about our need for re-housing. To date we seemed to have lived the not so fairytale story of *The Three Little Pigs* with Dad playing the part of the 'Big Bad Wolf'. It may seem surprising that I can still have the odd, not unfriendly chat with him at the garden gate. He is and always will be my father, and I can only regret that it was necessary for us to do what we did about him.

A week later I was back for my scheduled admission to Blanchardstown Hospital. I had only just settled into my bed when RTE were on to me, warning me that the television camera crew would be in to do a news item on me the next day. Apparently the arrangements involved a lot of last minute phone calls between the RTE newsroom, the Eastern Health Board Press Office and the hospital authorities, with my Dublin friends acting as co-ordinators. Usually I was given a single room, but on this occasion I had to take my place, temporarily, in a ward full of very sick men. Initially there were doubts about allowing such a disturbance to take place, but the authorities were sympathetic to the cause. In any case, the event proved entertaining to those patients conscious enough to appreciate what was going on.

The filming of my first ever television appearance was made mid-afternoon, and though I was mighty nervous, the camera lied for once! That very evening, on Tuesday, 14th May, the feature was shown at the end of the RTE 1, *9 O'Clock News*. After the editing was completed, I made only a very short appearance, the rest of the item being taken up with diagramatic explanation of my illness and the mention of donor cards. It was tremendously exciting to watch myself on the television, surrounded by a gang of nurses, porters and patients who, like myself, could hardly wait for the main news items to be over!

Martin and Martine launched a big attack on all the national newspapers, and various Dublin-based journals. They spent a day calling around their city offices, armed with copies of a very professionally-prepared press release and some good photos. It was noticeable that those papers whose reporters they met in person, responded by publishing articles, while those whose journalists were out of their offices ignored the press release.

A journalist and photographer were dispatched to my hospital bed by *The Evening Herald*, on 17th May, which was my twenty-fourth birthday. Martine was just coming down the corridor as the lady journalist was leaving. Both girls recognized each other instantly. By coincidence they had both worked together for a short while in the same library branch! My own, very true, words were quoted in this paper, "It would be the best present I could ever hope for – a heart and lung transplant would change my life." Everybody made a great fuss over my birthday, but I still wait hopefully for that magnificent gift.

It was a great boost to my morale seeing the articles appear one by one, day after day. *The Evening Herald* did a backpage feature, and produced a follow-up article a few weeks later which highlighted the proposal to shortly commence heart and lung transplantation in Ireland. Martin and Martine had no problem in persuading *The Irish Catholic* to devote its regular 'Eavesdropping' page to my story, as they happen to be friends of the editor, Nick Lundberg. Further coverage was gained in *Woman's Way* magazine, *The Cork Examiner*, and the Cavan provincial, *The Anglo-Celt*. One very kind anonymous donation of forty pounds was sent to Martine, whose address had been quoted, and this was lodged to my appeal account which had thus far lain almost empty. Notwithstanding all of this glowing limelight, wherein the world shared the knowledge of my plight, I alone had still to bear the pain and suffering of my unrelenting illness.

Towards the end of my hospital stay, when everything seemed to have petered out, a nice surprise came in the form of a phone call from Brenda Donohoe of *The Gerry Ryan Show*, which is broadcast on Nationwide 2FM morning radio. "Could you be ready to talk to Gerry and myself at 9.00 a.m. tomorrow, Brendan?" "Course I could, darlin'", said I in earnest. Brenda told all of Ireland about my 'beautiful blue eyes', and ever since that, I keep checking in the mirror in case they change colour and disappoint any attractive members of the opposite sex! Everything was timing itself beautifully; the letter to Gerry's show had been posted a month previously.

The most spectacular bit of journalistic art came as part and parcel of the Gerry Ryan connection. Just after the radio talk a duo arrived from *The Star* tabloid. They gave me an entire 'Page 3', and produced a brilliant colour photo of me being supported horizontally by a team of radiant nurses, while I gave the thumbs up signal. The title was inspired by this book – which I was working on then: '*THE WILL TO LIVE*'.

Inspired by their achievements thus far, Martin and Martine dared to show their faces again at the RTE studios in Donnybrook, with a view to chancing their arm at getting me on one of the television chat shows. However, this time they were confronted by some very patronising security guards who pulled across a ribbon of red tape to impede their progress towards the public reception area. The men in question admitted that they knew what my friends were about, and that it was all in a very good cause. But, they would have to phone somebody inside to gain access. This, my friends did from a public payphone half a mile down the road, much to the puzzlement of a programme researcher who never knew such rules to apply. In any case, their renewed efforts provided no immediate results as the season of television shows was coming to a close.

A couple of days before discharge, the doctors gave me a bleeper to bring with me everywhere I went, so that I could be paged in the event of donor organs becoming available. The acquisition of this gadget was an auspicious occasion as it signified just how close the greatest event in my life might be.

One week after I got back home to Ballybofey two very important and welcome visitors arrived on my doorstep. One was a fellow Donegal man, none other than the international Country and Western star, Daniel O'Donnell. Frances, managed to get Daniel's autograph, and I reckon my sister was sorry to hear shortly afterwards that the man announced publicly his betrothal to another. My other caller was Fr. Brian D'Arcy, a prominent journalist priest and member of the Passionist Fathers. Mother didn't know who next to expect up for tea!

11

___

AUGUST WEEKEND 1991

All through my life the long and winding road from Ballybofey to Sligo has been for me a route to hospital. Now, in my twenty-fourth year, I had at last experienced it as a happy and special journey. On the August Bank Holiday of 1991 my Dublin friends took the opportunity to visit me at home. Martin and Martine arrived to find me reasonably well and suggested taking Mother and myself out and about for the day. The limits imposed by the range of my bleeper restricted plans for our day trip. Martine took a map from her car and we laid it out on the kitchen table, observing the possibilities for an itinerary. The long and winding road seemed to be the only feasible choice, but God, did I know it only too well. Yet, I knew my friends were full of imagination and could make a novelty out of anything. When Martine put the question to me as to where exactly I'd like to stop off along the road I replied, "Darlin', you think of somewhere and I wont argue so long as it's not my old 'holiday home'." Of course, I was referring to Sligo General.

The day started off fine, but turned out wet. The long and winding road exists only in my memory. Four years previously the authorities straightened and widened it into a racetrack which by-passes some of the villages now only visited by those whose business takes them there. Martine knew where she was going as she sped along the road, the first raindrops of the day spraying a fine mist on the windscreen. I hadn't a clue where we might end up, though I guessed it might be somewhere a little off this beaten track. My privilege was to sit in the front seat of the little Austin Metro, whilst Mother and Martin kept each other company in the rear. Though I had taken a travel sickness tablet I kept wide awake and alert to all that passed before and behind my eyes. When he wasn't taking video shots of the passing scenery, Martin dozed off to sleep on Mother's shoulder, only to be awakened by my loud remarks. I enjoy keeping people alert!

After three quarters of an hour, Martine turned off the main road. We found ourselves driving through leafy lanes, trying to dodge potholes which had now become rain-filled and almost invisible. The occasional jolt didn't turn my stomach as it might have on less happy travels. The territory was becoming vaguely familiar to me as we headed into a remarkably beautiful valley, circumscribed by flat-topped mountains whose bare-rocked cliff tops peered down over slopes clothed by dark green conifers. It reminded me of the Nordic jigsaw scenes I had many times assembled. This was for real.

Soon, a lake appeared on our right; a long and glassy sheet of water which filled the centre of the glen. We pulled into a car park from where we walked towards a ravine, ushered by the hiss of falling water growing louder and stronger as the rain fell lightly around us. I summoned all the strength I could to help me walk up some steps. I had been here before, some twelve years ago on that well-remembered outing from Sligo General. As a child I had not the immense appreciation for the beauty of the place that I do now. Back then, I was more interested in the devilment I could make with my friend, Thomas. Still, the mischievous child inside me has never left. He runs alongside me all the time and refuses to let go. Standing by Glencar Waterfall I shifted my gaze past the white cascade and up onto the craggy rock-walled mountains. "Boy, that would be some fall you'd get from there, dead as a doornail without a doubt. No good to me, poor sod. Just think of the state of the body!" My companions laughed at my macabre sense of humour.

We continued on our way around the other side of the lake, taking in a distant view of the waterfall. Martine commented that this was 'Yeats Country'. She had read a little about it in a guide book from the library where she works. I don't care much for poetry myself, but I have learned to believe that a man named W.B. Yeats is Ireland's greatest dead poet . Apparently this area inspired him to some degree, and I suppose if you're a poet it surely would. What loomed in front of me now was not poetry, though. The new part of Sligo General caught my eye as it raised its ugly head on the approach to town. Behind it lies the old prison-like edifice, where I had spent a lot of time as an inmate. The new building is high and I reckon the patients must have a feast of a view, not that I envied them in the least. For a while I thought Martine was going to drive me up to the place to annoy me, but she switched track back onto the Yeats trail.

We must have taken a couple of wrong turns; at least, that's what Martine's occasional swear word led me to believe. I couldn't have cared less where we went as I was enjoying every moment spent going somewhere different. Another lake came into view, this time the larger expanse of water known as Lough Gill. The next stop was at a castle which I again recognized. "This time I'm going into that castle, or you wont be dragging me back into that car!" Mother grinned and my friends gave me an odd look. I told them about the day Thomas and I were here the castle was closed to the public. We paid our entrance fee and proceeded to explore Parkes Castle.

As we walked across the courtyard I wondered how many skeletons lay beneath the stones on which we trod, all that now remains of slain invaders of the fortress in the days of old. At least in 1991, we were welcome visitors and the worst fate that might befall us would be if our chauffeur twisted her ankle on the steps or stones. Mother ushered us into the forge house and explained to our Dublin friends how horse shoes were made. There were some inviting steps and spiral stairways leading to higher areas of the castle but I declined temptation in case I ran short of puff and got dizzy at the top! Martin made several attempts to lure me into an audio-visual show which was just about to take place indoors, but I pretended not to notice him as I hadn't yet seen all I wanted to see of the real thing. Not until I had done my little walkabout did I acknowledge his suggestion to view the next showing. This proved to be a most interesting and colourful piece of education, highlighting the rich heritage of ancient monuments in the area as well as telling us more about Parkes Castle. A lot more entertaining than what I remember of school lessons. Looking at the many children sitting quietly in the room, I wondered if they thought the same.

We were just about to leave the place when Martine did something to turn my cheeks bright red. The visitors' book at the reception desk had caught her eye and she indicated that I should sign it, whereupon she asked the castle guides if they they had heard about "Brendan McLoughlin, the lad from Donegal who will hopefully be the first patient to undergo a heart and lung transplant in Ireland". They had remembered seeing something about me on the *RTE News*. A long conversation ensued. I became aware of heads turning from all directions, some overseas visitors among the folks earwigging the banter. When we finally settled back into the car Martine commented on how pleasant the toilets were!

Lough Gill soon disappeared from view as we headed towards the village of Dromahair. This place reminded me of an English style settlement, though I had never been to England, or anywhere outside of Ireland for that matter. Most of my travels have been made sitting in front of the television, looking through picture books or constructing jigsaws, and every glimpse I get of a corner of my real world brings me miles further. Dromahair is very pretty, with gable-fronted houses and some half-timbered buildings.

It was a fair while before we saw the lake again. All along the route were signposts indicating places that appear in Yeats' poems, such as 'Dooney Rock' and 'The Lake Isle of Inishfree'. Some day, if I have the mind to, I might read over the poems, though I believe they don't dwell too much on scenic descriptions. The woods near the lake shore are very beautiful, though I imagine they would be truly majestic with sunlight filtering through the tall trees. We had to contend with the watery side of perfection.

The next stop we made was a place I had never been to before: the holy well of Tobernalt which nestles snuggly in a dark ravine. The water bubbles gently from beneath the ground and is reputed to have special powers. I believe that favours may be granted through an act of faith, a belief that God will listen kindly if you trouble yourself to ask Him in a special moment or place that is put before you. As Mother didn't have an empty bottle that she could fill with the water to bring home (and the only thing Martine had in the car was a half-filled can of oil) she blessed me with the water, saying a few silent prayers. Above the well is a grotto with statues of Jesus and Our Lady; most awe-inspiring of all were the myriad rows of tiny candles piercing the darkness from where the figures stood watching over us.

The return journey home brought us through the heart of Sligo town, which was quiet of a Sunday. Mother didn't recognise the place as she had spent all her visiting time in Sligo up at the hospital with me. Past the town we gathered speed on the 'highway' and Martine played a tape of Sixties music to pass the time. Mother was familiar with the tunes and their lyrics, having heard them in her younger days. Indeed she sometimes came out with me if there was a Sixties disco on in town and I almost had to pretend not to know her! Martine turned down the volume so as to cut out the noise of heavy breathing when 'Je t'aime' was playing. I don't know French, but it's not difficult to guess how the lyrics translate. And that heavy breathing is not due to lack of oxygen! Martin was fast asleep in the back and Mother was beginning to join him. I again shouted "Wake up boy, you're not going off on me!"

When we arrived back at the house my tummy was admittedly a little queasy, and I could not see myself looking forward to an evening out at the pub. My friends stayed in the car, saying they would call back for me at about 9.00 p.m. Mother went into the kitchen to prepare meals for the family while I took a little rest. No, I could not see myself being able for a night out, but my friends had come all the way from Dublin and I wished the day would never end for us all.

No time seemed to have elapsed when there was a knock at the door. My sister, Frances, had answered it and came up the hall calling me. In front of me now stood a very ashen looking Martin and Martine. Frances handed Martine a cigarette. Martin spoke quietly. "We've just been in with McGowans next door. Celia saw us on the road. We had a slight accident, skidded, and hit the ditch. Patsy is looking at the car." Martine was muttering something about going too fast, but said little else. Thankfully, neither of them was hurt physically, but it was obvious that they were in no fit state to go anywhere for the moment. The accident had happened only a minute after they had left us. Mother gave them both a small glass of potent liquor to steady the nerves, and some light nourishment.

The car was still driveable, though there was a fair bit of damage sustained as it had brushed against a stone wall. From our garden I saw it parked behind McGowans house, looking quite sorry for itself with the left-side rear window missing. Patsy McGowan, the father of the family, was taping on some clear plastic sheeting to cover the gap for the journey back to Dublin.

In the meantime Frances was preparing herself for a night out with her boyfriend. After completing each step in the process of grooming she would peep into the living room to see how our friends were, and maybe offer Martine another cigarette. The evening was wearing towards nightfall and Martine was anxious to drive back to the guesthouse before dark. Mother thought it would be better if the pair stayed the night with us, but most of their belongings were back at the guesthouse. Barely recovering from the trauma, they departed, promising to call in before going back to Dublin in the morning.

I went to bed immediately as I wasn't feeling too well. A good night's rest would do us all the world of good, I thought. Everything would be much better in the morning as the upset of the evening before would be sunk beneath the pillows. I slept fitfully as usual, being woken by the odd bout of coughing. By 1.00 a.m. everybody else was sound asleep as far as I could tell, except Frances who was out having a good old time of it. The dawn drew closer and closer and there was still no sound of her companion's car pulling in to leave her home. 'It must be a really good night for them' I thought, with a hint of envy. At 5.00 a.m. I was awoken by a subdued commotion in the hallway, and I came out to see what was going on. Lightning had struck twice. My poor sister had been involved in a skidding accident near Donegal town, but fortunately again, there were no physical injuries. She was extremely lucky, as not alone had the car been travelling at very high speed, but her seatbelt was faulty.

Later that morning, Martine and Martin called in, as promised, and were very surprised at the news. Apparently they had heard of other local road accidents that night from their landlady, though only one of them resulted in injury; the victim having suffered serious eye damage. Before our friends left, Mother got my younger sister, Martina, to write out a special prayer for them both, to protect them from any physical harm on their travels. She also requested that they phone us on their safe arrival back in Dublin. At 6.00 p.m. we received the happy call.

The next day we got some really good news, an answer to one of our prayers. The county council had finally granted us the house we longed for. It was the end of a journey of hope and now we had arrived at our destination; a home right in the heart of town. No hills for Mother to have to push my wheelchair up, I could perhaps even walk myself to the nearest shops or pub. Dad wouldn't be passing our way every day, and even if he troubled himself to come our way there would be too many townsfolk around to disturb him. The keys were delivered mid-afternoon.

12
—

THE SKY IS NOT THE LIMIT

At the time Mother planned our 1991 summer holiday to Bundoran it did not look like being a great idea. There was no knowing whether or not I would be laid up in hospital for treatment or assessment, and besides, my health was declining to such an extent that not a day would pass without some kind of alarm. Major seizures of coughing could overcome me at any moment, especially if I became physically or emotionally upset to any degree. Anywhere I might go for more than a day's outing meant that my medical equipment, including portable nebuliser, had to come too.

Less than a fortnight before our scheduled departure date we had got word of our imminent change of address, and God knows this would entail an enormous amount of planning and hard work in itself. For my sake, and that of my sisters, Frances and Martina, Mother insisted on going ahead with the holiday. She had invited our Dublin friends to spend at least part of the week with us, but only Martine was able to come, and only for just a couple of days at that, because of repairs that needed to be done to her car after the crash. The four of our family travelled to Bundoran on Saturday 19th August; Martine joined us the following Tuesday evening.

On the Monday morning I developed a very high temperature and had recourse to visit the doctor who was conveniently located across the road from the cottage which we had rented. Mother feared that I might have to 'enjoy' a two-centre vacation, the second being the not far off Sligo Hospital. Thankfully this did not happen, though the wretched fever continued through the night and into Tuesday. Frances and Martina urged me to get well for Martine's arrival, and reminded me of my duty to show her around my favourite haunts in the seaside resort. With all the encouragement given, I rallied just in time to don my shades and sun hat and set out up the town with Mother wheeling me.

We had arranged to meet in Brian McEniff's Holyrood Hotel, a venue familiar to all of us. As Mother pushed me up the entrance ramp I could see Martine coming to greet us across the foyer. She swiftly pulled off my cap and asked me, "Where are we going tonight, Bren? "Hold on a second, darlin', we're going walkies by the sea before we let you loose on the town!" said I, as she took control of my chair. I winked at Mother, knowing how awkward the Bundoran pathways are for pushing wheelchairs around. For a start, she nearly sent me leaping out of my seat at the end of the ramp. She was the one who got the fright though, as I am well used to keeping my placement from past experiences of malicious attempts to derail me.

Mother pointed our direction towards the beginning of the cliff walk as she told Martine of an incident two nights earlier when a policeman reprimanded us for jaywalking. We had asked the good garda whether he ever had the experience of negotiating a wheelchair on footpaths just broad enough for dogs to pass single file, not to mention the numerous steps and other obstacles that made the task slightly impossible? He was not too charmed, pointing his finger at Mother for having twelve-year-old Martina out at such a late hour. I was on my way home from a disco in Pepe's Nightclub, trying to lead the life of a normal young man. Mother tried explaining the circumstances, and informed the garda that she would not be so irresponsible as to leave her young daughter by herself in the house.

"Don't let me catch you again" was the gist of his reply. I think Martine was disappointed that she never got to meet this guardian of the law, although as she said, it might be more appropriate to address the county council who forced us into jaywalking in the first place.

Shortly, we came upon the main beach area, and the funfair amusements where my sisters spent much of their time. Also located here, is the newly opened 'Waterworld' where you can while away a wet day getting wetter. No better place if you're fond of swimming as the beach can be a treacherous place to take a dip. The red danger flag was waving about in the warm evening breeze, a gentle wind hardly responsible for the breakers which sabotaged the empty sands. A life-guard watched vigilantly in case anyone should venture towards the surf, but most were safely up in the town. A fortune-teller's booth caught Martine's eye, but she had gone off duty at that hour of the evening. Mother and I had visited her in previous years, getting told a little 'truth' amid the nonsense. I doubt if it takes a great deal of psychic talent to proclaim: 'difficulties in the past' and that 'things will get better in the future'. Still, £2 worth of hopeful inebriation sipped from Madame's words of comfort might last longer into the future than the cheer from a glass or two of the hard stuff.

We reached the more desolate stretch of the cliff walk, Martine and Mother having taken turns to wheel me uphill on the headland. I recognized the spot along these cliffs where we could view some spectacular rock formations. Here, I took to my feet, and asked Martine to follow me down the grassy slope, seawards. She seemed a little anxious about getting too close to the cliff edge, choosing to eye the seascape at a little distance. Mother came with me as far as the 'blow-hole' which lies just behind a rock archway known as the 'Fairy Bridge'. The sculptor responsible for this wonderful piece of masonry is the sea herself. She is a gifted artist, has hands that bear the thrust of her temperamental nature. She has a little way of telling you she doesn't like you; her victims have lungs wetter than mine! Mother and I had our eyes fixed on the blow-hole, waiting for a wave forceful enough to emerge upwards through it as a spectacular fountain. We asked her, "Blow, you bitch!", and she merely raised a small white eyebrow of surf against the precipice. Martine didn't get the thrill of witnessing a geyser of foam exploding through the hole.

Further along our way the golden sands of Tullan Strand stretched into the hazy distance. Chalky beige mountains of dune rise formidably behind, separating the lazy pleasures of sandcastle land from the military matters that are the business of nearby Finner Camp. My brothers and I used to tumble down these sandhills and play war games with water pistols. This evening the beach was empty, yet noisy with the thundering of waves marching soldier-like towards the shore in curious triangular convergence. Not one of us had a camera on hand to catch the glittering green translucence as the crests caught hold of the evening light.

Back amid the man-made cacophany of Bundoran town we gambled away £1.60 in the gaming halls. Each of us lent an arm in the operation of trying to seduce the one-armed bandits into giving us some money. One of us would hold the flowerpot of coins, one feed in the pennies and the other pull the lever. Lady luck was not on our side that night, which was a trifle embarrassing as I had boasted to Martine of our £20 win on a previous night. Before we left the premises we tried to persuade one of those 'cuddly toy' machines to kindly give us a furry friend to bring home to Martina, but again our luck was out. We took ourselves back to the house totally defeated.

Frances had spent the last two hours getting herself ready to come out with us for the night, so I guessed I could take at least an hour's rest before she would have her coat on. I would always keep a watchful eye on my kid sister at the disco, merely to tease the lass as she is more than able to take care of herself. By 10.00 p.m. we were inside the door of a local public house where furniture, fittings and customers merry, throbbed to the sounds of Irish songs. My mind travelled back to a night out I had with Martine and Martin in a Ballybofey bar, where they secretly conspired to have my name publicly announced by means of a request to the pub entertainer. Now I had the opportunity to get my own back on one of the pair responsible. An interval in the music prompted Martine to answer a nature call, and allowed me to approach the band with request for her. It was timed beautifully. As Martine emerged from the Ladies' toilet her name was announced loud and clear; we stood up and pointed towards her crimson face.

I know that alcohol was partly responsible for my friend's complexion because we ensured that this time her glass would be filled with more than just cola. Any time she had been with us before, her motor was parked outside, so until tonight I had only known a sober Martine – sometimes quiet but invariably ready for a bit of devilment. This night we were within walking distance, and not having to drive Martine could enjoy a drink. At pub closing time we headed on to the nearby disco.

Mother and Martina parted company with us at the entrance to Pepe's Nightclub; they would be returning at 2.00 a.m. to wheel me back to the house as was our usual arrangement. The minute the music started, Martine hauled me out onto a very empty dance floor, which I didn't mind in the least. It made a change from sitting in the corner, waiting for a group of familiar faces to arrive. With my condition you have to get to know people a little before you will be accepted to dance with them. As I have so little energy for moving to the beat of the music I need to explain the situation to potential dance partners. If I get too

Beside Malin Head, the northernmost point of Brendan's beloved Donegal

Brendan with Brenda Donoghue of the *Gerry Ryan Show*
(May 1991, Pre-Transplant)

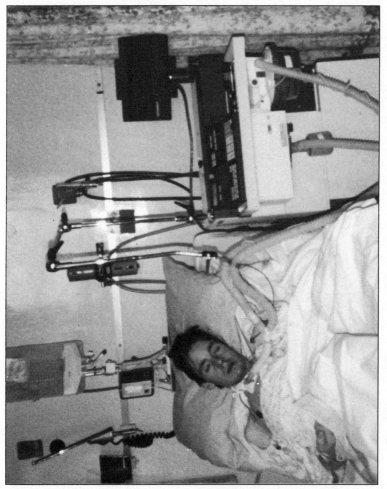

Brendan on life support in I.C.U. at Blanchardstown Hospital.
(July 1992, a month before his transplant)

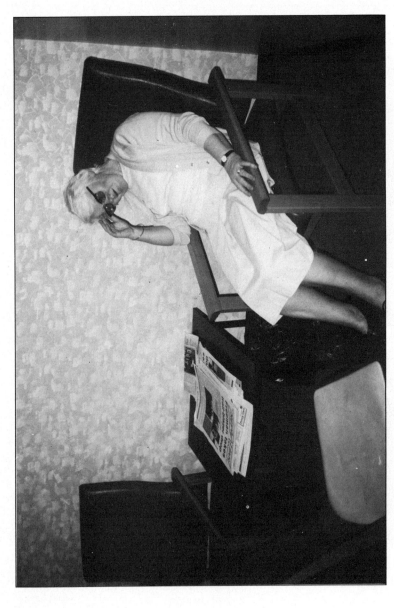

Frances McLoughlin, keeping vigil whilst her son, Brendan undergoes his lung transplant operation (10th August 1992, Freeman Hospital, Newcastle-Upon-Tyne)

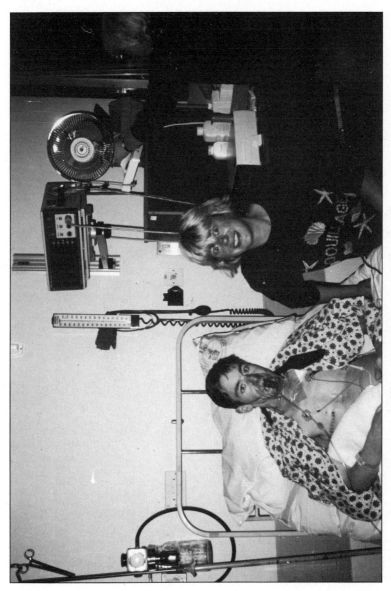

Brendan, 12 days after his lung transplant with a friend, Martine Brangan (22nd August 1992, Freeman Hospital)

Out of pyjamas (for the first time in 3 months) – Brendan begins his full recovery sporting a new tracksuit. (23rd August 1992, Freeman Hospital)

Martin Byrne (a friend) celebrates the success of Brendan's operation.

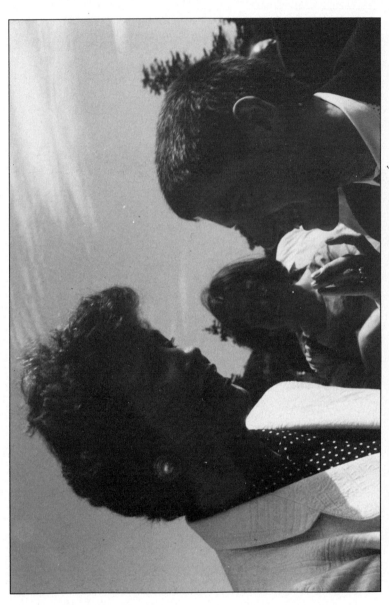

Brendan with President Mary Robinson on Family Day, 1993, at Áras an Uachtaráin (27th June, 1993)

exhausted I have to leave the floor which might otherwise cause misunderstandings. Tonight there was no question of that happening, I was so relaxed that I had more energy than usual. At one point our dance was rudely interrupted when one young man caught hold of Martine's arm. As she wasn't budging from her position he said, "Are you dancing with him?" He must have been very short-sighted as Martine suggested. She was enraged at his ignorance, but I told her to cool it, that people like that aren't worth the raised pulse.

Before closing time I settled myself into the wheelchair just inside the doorway, ready for Mother to arrive and have me out ahead of the 'rush-hour traffic'. Martine was well merry at this stage, full of enthusiasm and Dutch 'ability'. I said nothing, feeling a tinge apprehensive as she wheeled me out the door, manoeuvring her charge with surprising accuracy on the precarious Bundoran footpaths. I was only waiting for our garda friend to stop us and charge us with drunk driving. With some relief I saw Mother and Martina coming across the road to rescue me! My other sister was still back in the disco and the only one who slept through her noisy arrival back to the house was Martine. Exuberant Frances always managed to create an impromptu party, but none of us would dream of spoiling her fun for the sake of a bit more sleep.

I awoke quite early in the morning, but stayed beneath the sheets until some sounds of life gave me the signal to start preparations for breakfast. Martine was the first to emerge from her room and demanded a full-fried breakfast, egg to be done on both sides. She said she didn't mind burnt food so long as it was properly cooked. I told her I never burn food, that she would not have to suffer raw sausages either, and what turned out on her plate justified my little boast. "We have a day's journey ahead of us, this should suffice till dinner time." Where was she driving us this time, I wondered, thinking back to the August Bank Holiday trip.

She wouldn't give us a clue about our destination as we set off in the car from Bundoran. My sisters had opted to stay behind as there wasn't room for everyone in the small car. This time we enjoyed good dry weather that was not too hot. The 'inch of rain' which was forecast was to bide her time till nightfall. Ten minutes down the road Martine announced that we were going to visit her 'Auntie's lovely big stately home'. Martin once teased her for being a snob and she was playing up to this image for a laugh. Passing a gate-lodge we turned in to a big country estate with long narrow driveways leading through a dark forest, with delightful glimpses of the nearby sea. Finally the great mansion came into sight, in front of which we came to a halt. "Lissadell House is the name for your memoirs," Martine added that 'Lissadell Players' is the name of a drama group of which she was a member, and that put it in her mind to visit the house.

We joined an excellent guided tour of the interior, followed by a very large crowd of people, among them students of the Yeats Summer School. This classical Georgian mansion was the childhood home of Countess Markievicz and her sister, Eva Gore-Booth. Fascinating accounts were given of these two ladies and their father, Henry, who were friends of W.B. Yeats. Indeed, we were told, the house is still the home of the Gore-Booth family and not a state-owned shrine to our cultural heritage. Later on we were privileged to meet Aideen Gore-Booth, a fine old lady and descendent of Sir Henry, who listened to my story with great interest. In the music room our guide spoke of how the two famous sisters used to draw pictures when they were children, on the walls of this great room. I said that Mother would have killed any of us for doing that inside our little cottage at Carn, as I am inclined to say what I am thinking aloud, and and this raised many a laugh from the guide and company present. Mother is like me in this respect, too, and she couldn't silence her awe at the immense old gas-lit chandeliers. Neither of us had ever heard of Lissadell House before, and we had certainly never set foot inside such a place.

We indeed saw a lot of the house, maybe too much for my poor old lungs. There is an enormous staircase leading to a landing balcony, off which are situated the bedrooms. A big stuffed mousse's head grinned at me as I desperately tried to catch my breath half way up the stairs. I had decided to leave the wheelchair back at the house that day as it is awkward to fit into a small car. I was reaching my limit of endurance, but somehow I had to carry on in case I would miss something. There were stuffed birds of every conceivable kind, including a white blackbird, of all things. Sir Henry broke the rules, I suppose, like myself. All these animals, we learned, were souvenirs of his 'amateur' explorations of hitherto little investigated parts of the world. The bedrooms themselves had four poster beds, which are in a way not unlike hospital beds in that privacy can be secured by pulling the curtains!

Down in the old billiard room we came across an antique wheelchair, which was very different from the modern article. For one thing, Mother found it much freer in movement than my last one. I didn't dare to sit in it, though going by appearance it looked quite comfortable. Apart from the fact that the dear old thing wasn't designed to fold up neatly, it didn't serve to impress me that pushchair engineering has greatly advanced since the 1800's. One thing I could be sure of is that I'd get some odd looks going out and about in a vintage chair!

We left Lissadell House with a feeling that our visit had been very welcome and worthwhile. Our guide enthusiastically assured his patrons of their contribution to the future of the mansion, and expressed his hope to see everyone call back some day. He also addressed me personally whereupon I assured him emphatically, "You'll see me back, and I'll be up those stairs in one breath!" When I do return, there will be some semblance to the television serial, *Brideshead Revisted.*

We journeyed on through a very prosperous looking area outside Sligo town. A long road broadened out on its approach to our next port of call, its flanks graced by well-kept lawns. A row of very new and sizeable detached houses almost posed as bleached miniatures of the great grey Lissadell. A sign ahead named the seaside village, 'Rosses Point' where we stepped out of the car to fill our lungs with some very strong sea air. It is a bracing, invigorating resort, a place to embrace the ever-changing views whichever way you turn your head to the wind. Surprisingly the sea is relatively tame here, and although these sands look a bit grey compared to the sands of Donegal, I understand the waters play host to safe, enjoyable swimming.

At Rosses Point, as well as almost everywhere you go in county Sligo, Ben Bulbin – queen of the table mountains – looms large in the landscape. But here she competes for attention with an interesting 'jigsaw' of features on the southern side of the bay. A lesser mountain, Knocknarea, is as far distant as the eye travels, a few miles across an inlet seemingly choked with islands. A funny, painted statue of a man points the way for ships to go to Sligo Harbour. I wondered if he could do with a nice cup of tea, or better still a hot whiskey, to warm his cockles! In much the same manner as the Metal Man, Martine pointed to Coney Island, telling us that we'd be going there tomorrow if we were up early enough next morning. I asked her if we'd be getting the boat from here, but only got the vague reply, "Not quite". There must be a fairly decent ferry service, I thought, looking at the signs of habitation on the isle. It took a few minutes to register that the more renowned Coney Island in New York was named after that little patch of Irish grass, beautiful as it is.

As we were in the vicinity, Mother dared to suggest we pay a visit to Sligo General Hospital. This time I quite liked the idea as it would give me the opportunity to let them know I was still around, though I was sure they had read it in the papers. Also there was the chance that we might be able to renew our acquaintance with Dr. Bell, who would undoubtedly be interested to know how I was doing. We entered through the new building which was a far cry from what I remembered of the place. It looked more like a hotel inside, than a hospital, though the tell-tale scent of disinfectant betrayed its true identity. There is a browse-through shop, a hairdressing salon, a restaurant you might choose to eat in, even a small fountain in the foyer. We sought directions to the paediatric unit where I used to stay, and yes, it was still in situ in the less modern quarters.

A dozen mistaken treks through inappropriate corridors and more direction asking finally led us to our target. We entered 'paeds' through the high-handled door which is so designed as to prevent the little patients from discharging themselves. To my eyes nothing had changed about the place, except the people and the cartoon characters that come and go through different eras. We passed the anonymous faces of the staff at the nursing station and went into the dayroom, where all that remained of faces of the past were a few evergreen creations of Walt Disney. The more recent orange and black striped Garfield cat posed smugly here and there, although his short lifespan had almost run its course. The Mutant Ninja Turtles were doing fair battle with the old puss, whilst the latest and the greatest Simpsons looked set to assert themselves in no mean way.

I checked the cupboards in deliberate search for schoolbooks but there were none to be found. Perhaps the present day teacher has new educational methods, or maybe she has a photographic memory for book pages! There were games aplenty: Scrabble, Snakes and Ladders, all the old favourites. What was missing was the trace of a jigsaw. I don't think I would have been too happy about that in the old days. On the other hand, a television set is now to be found in each ward.

As we went back into the corridor a nurse asked, "Can I help you in any way?" I saw from her uniform that she was the Sister-in-Charge, and hers was at last a face I recognised. Introducing myself as a past patient was necessary, as she did not recall ever having me in her care. Back in those days she was a Staff Nurse and had of course seen many children pass through her hands over the years. She was honest about not remembering me, though she had actually read about a 'Brendan McLoughlin' in the local newspaper, who was writing his autobiography. When my ex-nurse discovered this hitherto 'stranger' was going to mention her in his book she expressed hope that I wasn't going to say anything bad about her. And now I have the opportunity to positively allay her fears. The lady has all the attributes that make an individual devote her life to the profession I unashamedly admire the most.

Apparently we had just missed Dr. Bell, by a mere thirty minutes. Although he is now working in England, he still has associations with Sligo General and comes back on visits. We bid farewell to all the friendly faces now gathered in animation, smiling at the banter between their Superior and myself. On the journey back to Bundoran I tried again to satisfy my curiosity about tomorrow's outing. Martine had told me she wouldn't be joining us in Pepe's tonight as she, being driver, needed to be fresh as a daisy quite early the next day while the rest of us could nod off if necessary in the passenger seats. I asked her why we would be chasing time so specifically and got the peculiar answer, "Low tide is around half-eleven". I could have annoyed her more, but that would have spoilt the mystery.

Thursday morning saw us back on the road again, this time with my twelve-year-old sister in tow. Frances opted to stay around Bundoran as she had made a few friends to hang about with. Martina was eager to join one of her 'almost namesake's' tours and indeed the similarity of names had already lead to embarrassing confusion from time to time. For example, when Mother shouted, "Get up you lazy thing, Martina!" – as if she would treat friends like that. Now, my little sister carried a notebook and pen with her, so she could take down very accurate notes for my memoirs whilst I could let the whole day float over me in blissful relaxation. Martina was doing 'reporter' for her own research too – school term was on the horizon and she wanted to show her teacher how much can be learned outside of the classroom. We often think she is cut out to be a journalist, but only time will tell.

I was cute enough to ask Martine to stop at the village of Drumcliffe, having remembered that the place was mentioned during our tour of Lissadell House. It is the place where W.B. Yeats lies in rest, in a churchyard nestling at the foot of Ben Bulbin. The flat-topped mountain was looking her best, palest blue in the mist. My sister quickly located the poet's grave and took note of his epitaph on the headstone, 'Cast a cold eye on life, on death. Horseman pass by.' Somehow I get a feeling that Yeats' mind operated in quite a different way to mine. Inside the church I signed the visitor's book, giving a brief account of my forthcoming operation. Ever since Parkes Castle I got into this little habit. God knows who might read it and pray for me, every hope counts. On leaving the place, Mother commented on how eerie the churchyard looked with its umbrella of dark gloomy trees. Some might call it peaceful, but I wouldn't have much peace of mind walking about here at midnight under a full moon!

A little later in our travels we came to a signpost for 'Coney Island'. As I had thought, Martine took this turn, looking at her watch to check the time. "Should be O.K." said she confidently. The mystery was soon uncovered when we beheld the miles and miles of bare brown sands that started where the road stopped. Martine began to have misgivings as she saw the big pools of water that lay in the course ahead which was marked by big stone 'monuments'. These stood erect from the sands, straight in a row as far as the eye could see. Coney Island was barely visible.

Martine got out of the car and walked out over the enormous naked beach, staring down into the pools to ascertain depth. A warning notice had suffered so much weather damage as to be unreadable. Two horse riders passed by, probably casting a cold eye on our trepidation. A land rover drove out off the beaten track, but we reckoned that to be a fit vehicle for such an act of daring. Then, at last, two real cars, one of them a BMW, made the journey following the markings. Martine summoned the courage to follow them. She drove slowly over the bumpy sands and pools. It took us about ten minutes to reach the island shore where we came in sight of the few houses there. Mother commented that our Frances would fair badly living here, depending on the tide as to whether or not she could go out to a disco for the night!

We didn't stop to explore the island as Martine wasn't going to risk the tide cutting us off. I wouldn't have minded in the least having to spend twelve hours here. It was quite peaceful. The return journey seemed a bit precarious as a film of water seemed to be rushing over the strand. Full speed windscreen wipers were needed to maintain any sort of visibility, it was as if we were going through a massive rainstorm. The waters would have to be coming in the window before I'd grow alarmed, but I tried my best to get Martine worried. If she was scared she didn't betray it at the time, but there was a telltale sigh of relief when we regained the tarmac on the mainland. A week later Martine reported a beach in the front drive of her Dublin home after three attempts to wash underneath her car.

A lay-by on the road to Strandhill gave us a bird's-eye view of where we had been. From here the sands seemed perfectly dry and they remained looking so for quite some time. It was the biggest beach I have ever seen in my life, named, I hear 'Cumeen Strand'.

Sligo Airport is the first and only aerodrome I had visited in my life. In fact I didn't even know they had one there until we came across the signpost. Mother had never seen an aeroplane in her whole life (except on television), her eyesight being too bad to have even caught a glimpse of one passing overhead. We drove into the car park which doesn't cost a penny to enter. It's only when you want to leave that you have to pay fifty pence! If the car were more versatile we would have considered exiting via the runway. Martine remarked that the terminal building is tiny compared to that of Dublin Airport, but adequately serves the few flights a day which link this region with Dublin and Britain. There were three check-in desks, for Aer Lingus, Ryanair and Dan Air respectively, and one of them was busy with a small queue of passengers. I envied just a little, their freedom to take off just like that.

Martine enquired when the next flight was due in, so that we could see a large aircraft close-up in all its glory. There was one toy-sized single propeller plane sitting all by itself on the tarmac, but we would have to wait almost two hours to see the Aer Lingus model. We were sitting in the lounge drinking coffee to pass the time when Martine apparently got a bit restless. She excused herself for a few minutes, the rest of us supposed she must be visiting the bathroom. Then I saw through the internal window that she was talking to an 'official' looking man, but couldn't think what she was up to. They were both looking in our direction. The door was slightly ajar, so I sharpened my hearing and caught the man's voice saying, "Does the child scare easily?" I heard Martine reply, "Actually, he's a twenty-four-year-old man, and it would take some doing to knock a feather out of him."

I immediately copped what was going on as I looked back out at the miniature aeroplane. It was something I'd never dreamt that I would do except possibly as part of a last minute semi-conscious journey to England for the big operation. The idea of me travelling in an aeroplane just for the sheer joy and fun of it was incomprehensible, yet it was going to happen today. Surely if this came about, anything wonderful could happen. Surely, I thought, the sky is not the limit!

The joyflight was arranged for 6.00 p.m., the earliest time any of the amateur aviators of Sligo Aero Club would be available to fly after their day job. I have learned that these pilots fly purely for the love of it and that all the payment goes to the Club for aircraft maintenance, fuel, insurance, and other such expenses. We had several hours to fill-in doing other things, but I was getting more and more excited by the minute. My cough, which had been quietly sleeping up to this, was re-awakening. My little sister suggested I warn the pilot beforehand in case he thought it necessary to make an emergency landing somewhere!

The fifty pence exit fee allowed us the freedom to drive down the road to Strandhill beach, which is backed by a steep slope of boulders. We collected a large number of these, in their varying shades of red and grey, with a view to making a rock garden in front of our new home. Mother had accumulated a ridiculous pile of them, wedged right up to her chin. I removed my old leather jacket and we carried them between us in that, which was much more practical. Martine had a single-handed go at lifting the bundle into the boot of her car, but my strong-armed mother had to come to the rescue. It's not hard to tell who was reared in the city!

We proceeded on to the prehistoric sight of Carrowmore, via a scenic road which hugs closely the foot of Knocknarea Mountain. The close-up view of its western side reveals a curiously stepped series of cliffs ascending to the summit, in contrast to Ben Bulbin whose single escarpment rises sheer from a concave slope. The ancient graveyard at Carrowmore, five-thousand-years-old and the second largest of its kind in Europe, lies within view of Knocknarea. The impressive gathering of lowland antiquities is echoed by a cairn located on top of the mountain which has the legendary name of Queen Maeve's Grave. Some day, when I am fit enough, Mother and I will climb up to see it. Today I had to contend with exploring the myriad stone circles and cairns which were dotted throughout fields recently acquired by the Board of Works. A visitors' centre has been set up here which, like Parkes Castle, offers a good audio-visual show in addition to a worthwhile exhibition which explains the history of the place.

There is an arrangement of stones on nearby private land which, according to traditional belief, cures a sick child if she or he passes through the 'archway' three times in succession. Unfortunately I didn't qualify for the cure, but back in the early days, had my ever-hopeful mother come upon this piece of information, I would undoubtedly have been encouraged to perform the ritual. In which case, no stone would have been left unturned!

As the appointed time for my excursion skywards was drawing closer we thought it wise to journey once more in the direction of Sligo Airport. We still had one more quick stop to make, as things turned out. While driving along the road we passed a thatched cottage museum and gift shop. Succumbing to the temptation, Martine did a U-turn and parked alongside a wall of pink flowers, outside 'Dolly's Cottage'. The lady in charge of this museum vowed to include me in a list of prayers that are said each week by a group of faithfuls in the local parish. The more I get around, the greater is the deluge of calls on my account to 'the Man Above'.

The airport was quiet this evening and the check-in desks were closed off by steel shutters. We hadn't stayed around to see the Aer Lingus flight come and go as there would be more than enough excitement surrounding 'the Brendan voyage'. At 5.45 p.m. a man appeared into the lounge, his white pullover covered in oil. With a gleeful smile he approached us and asked, "Now, would any of you fly in a plane with a man dressed like this?" I volunteered without hesitation. This jovial character introduced himself as Paul Mullen, and expressed feigned disappointment at the prospect of not having female company on board. "Well I hope you know something about flying aeroplanes because I'm just getting the grip of it myself," said Paul, with a worried look on his face. I knew I was in for an enjoyable experience; people like him make all the difference.

He went up to the bar counter and grabbed a quick cup of tea whilst making conversation across the room with a very serious looking German pilot. "Very tricky landing. The mountain is creating a lot of turbulence," our foreign friend remarked solemnly, his brows almost coming bumper to bumper in congested thought. "I can't wait to feel this turbulence, might be more fun than the sort I'm used to." My interjection didn't seem to impress the serious man. Paul grinned, left down his cup, and beckoned me to follow him. As I left the lounge Mother, Martine and Martina had assumed positions to gain full view of the outside world in case they missed anything.

Paul logged in a couple of details about our flight plan in the Briefing Room. After that it was out to the aircraft, a two-seater Cessna 150. Martina noted the registration, EI-BBN. I climbed into the tiny cockpit and occupied the right-hand seat, as instructed. Apparently the left seat is for whoever is in charge of the driving, although the controls are duplicated. Before taking his seat, my pilot walked around the plane checking all its little parts in case any might be less than airworthy. Having found everything to his satisfaction he ensured that we were both suitably restrained by lap and shoulder belts. This could come in useful in the event of us finding the ground where the sky had been.

Paul radioed the control tower for permission to start the engine, a practice which any car driver might find tiresome were such a road law to be introduced. With the key in the ignition, the propeller flickered in front of us, becoming invisible as the engine burst into life. More checks were made, and from these I learned that an aircraft engine is intrinsically less prone to breakdown than most car engines are. There are two ignition systems; if one fails the engine keeps going. And there are no radiator or hose pipes to leak. All of which is quite reassuring when one considers that there are no A.A. phones conveniently located in the sky.

Further permission was sought to get out as far as the runway. I began to get very pleasantly excited as I still couldn't quite imagine what it would be like up there. We passed a windsock which showed that the air current was drifting somewhat across the runway. Paul said that he would turn away northwards from Knocknarea to avoid much of the turbulence. Having 'backtracked' the runway, we turned around for take-off. Full throttle was set, we quickly gathered the speed of a galloping horse. Still feeling the grip of the tarmac we now bolted along and I was fully resigned to losing touch with the ground. Suddenly the 'grip' was lost and a saner sense of motion was felt. The runway was below us and I was flying.

A few bumps shook us as invisible air currents crossed our path, but true to his word, Paul banked the Cessna gently northwards, away from the eddies. We climbed out over Cumeen Strand and Coney Island. The engine buzzed away full pitch, though we appeared to be making less and less progress over the terrain. Everything below grew smaller and smaller, unbelievably so. We passed over Rosses Point and I could see clearly now its situation at the head of a peninsula amid the complex geography of Sligo Bay. Crossing another inlet, Paul pointed out Lissadell House. It looked like the model of itself which we saw exhibited in the Billiard Room. At this point I was told we were flying at 1,500 feet, the highest I have ever been on land or in the air.

To our right was the large group of limestone table mountains, incised by the U-shaped valley of Glencar. This time I was almost eye to eye with their 'tabletops'. I couldn't quite see the waterfall, but the lake was in full view. Beautiful as they were, we gave these hills a wide berth and headed back out over the wild Atlantic Ocean as far north as the seaside village of Mullaghmore. From there I could just about see the lights of Bundoran. I found it hard to visualise that my sister, Frances, was actually down there somewhere, probably doing her own bit of flying on the amusements. Little would she know her brother was part of that speck in the sky, were it to have caught her attention. Being so far removed from reality, I couldn't think now that I'd be down below in Pepe's tonight. I couldn't even remember what being on land was like.

We made a tighter turn of 180 degrees to head directly back to base. The world almost turned on its side, but I had total confidence in the calmly executed manoeuvres of my expert pilot. Immediately below to my left was the coastline, fringed with white specks of diminutive waves. How much more threatening these enormous breakers look when you stand soberly beside them! As we descended on our approach to the airport the reality of the earth's surface gradually came back to my consciousness. A few pockets of turbulence reflected the rippled contours of the water. The engine note diminished as the plane nosed slightly downwards. Our final turn aligned us with the black runway ahead which for a while seemed to stay fixed in a distant view. Quite unexpectedly it came in front of us, large as life, swaying a bit. Paul cut the engine to tickover as we floated for a few moments before gently nudging the solid ground. The most tremendous experience of my life was just behind me.

Paul let me taxi the aircraft from the runway to the parking area, known as the 'apron'. I was surprised to learn that on the ground an aeroplane is steered by the feet. Seeing the faces of my entourage pressed against the lounge window, Paul flashed the landing light twice. When we rejoined them indoors, my little sister came forward with a postcard of the airport that she had just purchased. She asked Paul to autograph it and he looked somewhat surprised. "Am I famous or something?" he mused whilst obliging Martina. She examined his signature and read out what was written underneath, 'C.F.I.'. With a little encouragement, Paul abandoned his natural modesty in telling us that he was Chief Flying Instructor of both Sligo and Donegal Aero Clubs.

Before departing for Bundoran by less exotic means of transport, Mother and Martina had a chance to look around the Cessna 150. My sister sat in the cockpit and asked Paul all sorts of involved questions about the controls and instruments. She was enthralled at the idea of taking a flight, but there was no possibility of that happening today. Mother made a promise to her that her wish would come true some day in the future. And a promise made by our mother is not a litany of empty words.

Everyone was ushered indoors as an Aer Lingus training flight was on the approach. The runway became ablaze with lights to guide in the new Saab aircraft. We were, afterall, fated to see in life-size proportions a real passenger aeroplane.

Martine, on her last day with us, let us into a secret. Quite a few years ago she used to take flying lessons in Dublin, and had some solo experience. She was forced to give up her Student Pilot's Licence for reasons relating to her eyesight, but has never lost her fascination for aviation. Apparently, whilst working together in the same branch of Dublin Libraries, Martin and she were in the habit of making the occasional aerial sortie. As truths emerge, God only knows what other weird and wonderful surprises lie in front of me.

13

LOSSES AND GAINS

Almost immediately after returning from our 1991 holiday in Bundoran we moved into our two-storey council house in the town. The previous year our return was associated with the terrible tragedy of our neighbour's death; now we were to be parted from them, which was the only sad aspect of our move. Again it was a busy, though happier time of the year for us. This was just one week away from my next date for Blanchardstown, and little did I realise then just how long it would be before I would see our new home again. It was quite a novelty having two floors and a stairs to climb as we had always lived in bungalows. Of course, I could only manage the stairs very slowly and very occasionally, so I took over the downstairs! I was looking forward to being able to go out more frequently as all the amenities were virtually on the doorstep. When I left for Dublin the place was in a state of utter chaos, and I had to use my imagination to picture it as a cosy family residence.

On 9th September I travelled to the hospital in the company of my mother and two sisters who were both to be investigated by Dr. Burke because they suffered recurring chest infections. It happened that we had the ambulance transport to ourselves, which made for a memorable journey, with the frolics of vivacious teenage Frances proving to be a greater driving force than any engine. She didn't like hospitals, or the thought that she might be ill, and this was her way of coping with it all. When we got to Blanchardstown the party ambience continued in my room and the jollity endured late into the night, after

Martin and Martine came in to visit. Frances always loved to tease the men, so Martin had his head, arms and legs twisted every which way she could without doing serious damage!

On my second day 'in residence' at the hospital I was delivered some very surprising news. A sweat test which was done on me two months previously proved positive – I had cystic fibrosis. My sister, Frances, was shortly to find out that she did too, and Martina was also under investigation. We had a hereditary disease, acquired at conception by the meeting of two faulty genes, one from both our parents. Cystic fibrosis is a 'recessive' genetic disease – if you have one faulty gene you don't have the disease, if you have two you do. If you have one or two of these genes you can pass it on to your children, if your partner carries the gene also. So, your parents can be perfectly healthy and have no reason to suspect that their children won't be too, unless they know already that C.F. cases have appeared somewhere in the extended family. Knowledge is presently increasing, not so long ago premature deaths in rural areas were likely enough to be put down to all sorts of vague things. Typically, we had no knowledge of C.F. having occurred before.

A sample of our mother's blood was taken to confirm that she carried the gene, and sent to Belfast for analysis as we have neither a testing facility, nor genetic counselling, available in the Republic. It was logical that my father be tested likewise, but the difficulties that beset getting his co-operation ruled this out. Frances was naturally upset to think that not alone did she have the damned illness, but could pass it on to her children if she was unfortunate enough to marry someone who carried the gene. She was thinking to herself, 'Does this mean I have to ask my next boyfriend to be tested in case we fall madly in love and want to get married?' Likewise, any of the healthy members of my family could be carriers as well. I, at least, don't have that anxiety as I am sterile like most males with C.F.

Now that I was once again one of their own, I made contact, through Martine, with the Cystic Fibrosis Association. There was a postal strike at the time, so that she personally delivered my letter and officially signed doctor's certificate' to their office in the Dublin suburbia. They spoke to Martine and gave her a host of highly enlightening literature to pass on to me. Not only that, but one of the C.F.A. people came out to visit me, to ensure that I was faring as well as I might.

Another thing that came as a surprise was that I was not on any transplant waiting list that was likely to fulfil my hopes. Earlier in the year I had been given to expect that the government was just about to give the go-ahead for heart and lung transplants to be performed in Dublin's Mater Hospital, but apparently the decision had now been postponed indefinitely. I had not been assessed in any British centre, which I learned meant that in effect I was not in any queue at all. I had thought that my Irish assessment details were good for Britain too, but how wrong I was! My ignorance was bliss, I was surviving on hope. My mother and I were discussing all this with the doctors, and her words left them in no doubt as what to do next. "I want a living son, not a dead hero!" she exclaimed to nodding heads who agreed to make contact with the Freeman Hospital in Newcastle-Upon Tyne, one of the British transplant centres which also includes Harefield, Papworth and Great Ormond Street.

In the room next to me was a very seriously ill patient who groaned audibly day and night. I was assured that he wasn't expressing pain, that it was just his disease triggering off the part of the brain that controls the vocal cords. (I'm not sure that I believed that.) One of my healthier fellow patients, a very nice man who used to come in for a chat with me, sympathised with my having to listen to the vocals next door. I told my friend that I didn't mind in the least, after all, anyone could be like that some day and I would like to think that no one else would regard me as a disturbance. My friend agreed. In any case, the moaning stopped a couple of days later and I never heard whether or not it was because the poor man died.

On a happier note I got word that I had a date to appear on *Kenny Live* , the Saturday night television chat show . This was as a result of renewed efforts by the ever-persistent Martin and Martine. It was not established if I would be on the platform or in the audience on 16th November, but I learned that the main part of the scheduled feature was to be devoted to a girl named Gillian Staunton who had undergone a heart and lung transplant and was at this time doing very well. Very sadly, in September 1993 gillian passed away. She had developed complications and was put on a waiting list for a further transplant, but didn't live to see this happen. She was a very active girl right up to the last, and as her mother Veronica stated in the paper, Gillian had 'three wonderful years.' According to her will, to donate her eyes, Gillian gave the gift of sight to someone blind.

The idea of meeting a thriving recipient was exciting enough let alone the thought of Pat focussing attention on me. I quickly let word spread around the hospital of my forthcoming first, live appearance on television. One of the staff nurses, Geraldine, revealed that she was to be wed on that date. No doubt she would be having other things on her mind that night!

My sense of humour had an opportunity to express itself one evening when Martin came in with a pair of theatrical wigs. We both placed these artificial crops of profuse long, wavy hair which made us look like a pair of hippies, on our neatly tailored domes. It altered our appearance so much that Martine, who was arriving later, thought she had entered the wrong room. We managed to fool some of the nurses, but word had got around to the remainder who were sent in to see the spectacle.

On the home front a pathetic situation occurred involving Bord Telecom who were threatening to cut off our phone, claiming that Mother had omitted to pay for connection charges. Some clerical error was at hand, causing a lot of unnecessary distress at a time when we could do without that kind of thing. Mother had to remind them that the phone was now absolutely essential, her only means of knowing how near to death's door her son was. The doctors had ordered the phone to be there in the first place, it was totally absurd to think that anyone else had the authority to take it away again. Thankfully the problem was settled before our vital line of communication was wilfully cut.

I was on the usual I.V. antibiotic treatment, which normally got the chronic infection under control for another while. This time, instead of getting better I was getting worse. I was spitting up lots of very dark, brown-coloured mucus, getting sicker and weaker, and my temperature was peaking. I was told that I had double pneumonia. The oxygen I was on was increased from twenty-four to twenty-eight per cent, and I had to breath this in through a mask for sixteen hours a day. Five different antibiotics were administered to try and combat the infection, but none of them seemed to be working. Blood cultures were taken constantly; medications were given through every route, including my rectum. Repeated bronchoscopies were performed in an effort to clear my lungs of the pints of fluid that were forming on them. I could no longer make it to the phone when Mother called every second night. When she managed to come down from Donegal again she was shocked to see how much worse I had got since she saw me last.

My Dublin friends issued another press release about my latest deterioration, and grim reports soon followed in *The Evening Press, The Star,* and *The Evening Herald.* Back in Donegal, Chris Ashmore of *The Donegal Democrat* wrote a series of features about my progress, or lack of it. He was frequently on the phone to Mother and Martine, expressing a deep personal concern for my welfare. I was now far too ill to travel to Newcastle for assessment, even if they had a bed for me, but renewed appeals for my fund were made in the hope that it would some day be used. Thus far, the response had been very poor, not surprising as we had been reluctant to hold out the begging bowl.

I was becoming more and more detached from the world around me as soaring temperatures stole part of my consciousness. The only thing I could completely feel were the overwhelming pains that tore through my guts. Having read the C.F. leaflets I realised these were exacerbated from not having been put on digestive enzymes. My intestines couldn't cope with the food and it all too readily manifested in my low state of health. I asked one of the doctors on duty to right the situation, to put me on the enzymes. He ordered a stool test to be done which showed that fat was passing through me, totally undigested. He put me on enzymes, a more suitable diet was implemented, and from then on at least I did not have abdominal agony to contend with.

I was now on the critical list, with one foot in the grave. One dreadful night I can barely afford to think about, I was on the verge of putting my other foot in there too. Martine and Martin were at my side, though I could barely see them. They touched me, held me. I was terrified, I didn't want to let go, couldn't afford to let myself lose contact. I felt my eyes closing to the hazy figures leaning over me. This was the darkest hour in the darkest night. Almost invisible vapours of light still remained, and I knew somehow I could make it if I tried hard enough. *The Will To Survive* had to be my trump card. My eyes shut, my eyes opened; reality was lost, then regained. I remember saying, "That's not sleep coming on." It was as much as I could say. Voices whispered and surged. Sometimes I could hear the noise of a fan which was blowing currents of air to cool my overheated body. All the strength in my mind was relayed to my hands in sporadic efforts to clutch the hands of my two living friends. They had spoken to the nurses and were expecting the worst.

Mother was notified about my condition and made immediate plans to come down on the next available transport, which was next morning. She was distraught to think that I could be dead before she'd make it down. All she could do that night was hold a prayer vigil around a lighted candle with family, supported by our great local friend, Sarah McNulty.

I did make it through the night, I have survived to tell the tale. Mother was now at my side for the next few difficult days. I was extremely weak, helpless to the point where I could do absolutely nothing for myself. This was quite depressing for me but I knew I couldn't ponder on these thoughts as it would destroy my willpower to fight, something I had built up over twenty-four years of struggling for life – especially with the likelihood of a transplant coming in the not too distant future. Martin and Martine were visibly worried, but I reassured them that with the help of God I could make it through this bad patch, knowing that I was at all times stronger than my illness. This, my mental strength, I find to be the most important weapon in the art of survival; if you never give up you will never lose.

The portable television set that Mother brought down from home gave me something to occupy myself with, helping to me to pass the long helpless hours. My brother, Seamus, was now doing construction work on Trinity College in Dublin, and was thus able to visit me often. I felt I was improving slowly, very slowly. Pressure sores had now become a problem, affecting my private parts, after six weeks of being largely confined to bed. I had bad headaches from sinusitis, and a peptic ulcer which re-kindled itself. Some things were getting worse while other things improved, and I was still very much in the woods. The most distressing bouts of coughing imaginable were racking my body. I screamed the place down in an effort to try and suppress the choking ordeals. There was no breath left in me afterwards, and I was desperately anxious that one of these attacks might try to kill me.

Frances was admitted to the hospital for a few days for a check up, and to start enzyme treatment. She was terrific, a lovely sister to have at my side during my bad moments. She had a special way of getting me through them, of being in control with the most gentle but firm manner. We were both in the same boat, with my end taking in water, but Frances was the captain and would not let us capsize. Typically she might say, "Toad, you get your act together, get your rotten old lungs to breathe easy," and I would reply, "Maggot, I have no lungs to breathe with!" Then she would argue with that, and win. When her day to be let home came around she refused to leave, and stayed with me for another while, until the worst of my coughing episodes were over.

I saw my youngest sister, Martina, again when she came down with Mother for another sweat test. The last one proved negative in spite of her presenting with milder symptoms of the disease. She is a happy, intelligent, lovable little girl, and we awaited the results of the latest test anxiously . Sadly, it proved she had C.F.

A national bus strike caused problems for Gerard, who was very concerned to see me after so many weeks separation. Eventually he managed to travel down late in the evening on a private bus, and the nurses allowed him to break the rules and visit me from 10.00 p.m. till after midnight. Kevin, our talented cookery expert, was working in a hotel which involved weekend duty, so I insisted that he should not try and see me. I was getting over the worst of my infection, which turned out to be a fungus which had caused bad consolidation of my lungs. An anti-fungal drug was winning the battle.

Eight weeks in hospital, and my oxygen was reduced back to twenty-four per cent. My temperature had gradually stabilised, the drugs, drips and machinery were much less in evidence. Seamus, my supplier of all things good and delicious, brought in cans of Guinness which I relished and thrived on. My mother and family at home rejoiced when I made my first phone call to them in a long time. It was proof that I was coming around. The best news yet was when Dr. Burke told me that he had got the green light for my assessment in England. It was just a matter of about two or three weeks before I would be sent over.

My date for *Kenny Live* was nearing, and it looked like I was going to be fit enough to appear. Throughout my severe infection I had promised myself that I would fulfil this appointment. But now it looked like my plan was going to be thwarted again, not due to illness, but as a result of arrangements for that night's show being under review. I watched the next week's show on my little television set, and could taste it, feel it, imagine my presence there. There was still a chance that I would be on, but apparently that was growing slimmer.

In the meantime I had a rare visit from my father. Mother had thought that he had a right to see his sick son, and Dad agreed that he should do just that. We had a long, amicable chat about my forthcoming trip to Newcastle, and my hopes for the near future. He promised to keep in touch with my progress. It was quite a change for him travelling up to Dublin, but our mini-bus driver friend, Joe Francie Marley, looked after him well on the trip.

On Friday 15th November I got a phone call from Martine that I was, after all, to be on *Kenny Live* the next day! Two audience tickets were being made available, one for myself, and one for a companion. I would be given the opportunity to say a few words during the feature where heart and lung transplant girl, Gillian Staunton – fellow C.F. sufferer – would be 'on stage' with her mother, talking to Pat. Her mother had written a book about her experiences leading up to, during and after the operation, entitled *Gillian: A Second Chance*. At that time I was writing this and was naturally enough interested in her book which was about to be launched. The doctors and hospital staff were delighted to be able to release me for the show, but of course I had to be accompanied by one of the nurses. Martine was to be our chauffeur for the occasion, and unfortunately, although she and Martin had arranged the whole thing, neither were to be in the audience with me. Martin couldn't even be with us as he had a cold and was in danger of passing on the infection to me.

The next evening, Saturday 16th, I got out of my pyjamas and into 'civies' for the first time in ten weeks. There was a lot of slagging and teasing, and great excitement. The only thing to steal my thunder was that this was nurse Geraldine's wedding day, and most of the off-duty staff would be at the 'afters' that night. Tragically, Geraldine's happiness was to be followed by the most immense sorrow imaginable. Fate stuck a cruel blow when both her husband and their baby died unexpectedly in separate circumstances. Nurse Cathy was also dressed smartly in her 'civies', looking very unlike a nurse. She had volunteered to be my medically experienced guardian. Martine arrived in to collect us, all glam and wearing make-up for a change, just in case she got a last-minute chance to be seen on television.

We drove through Dublin city, I saw floodlit buildings as I've never seen them before. Ten weeks inside and you really notice the world outside in all its tangible glory. Driving through the main thoroughfare of O'Connell Street, people stepped out in front of us, sometimes coming close to being victims of their own stupidity. A row of little Christmas trees projected out from above the window of a big department store. Christmas! How near that was getting! We passed Trinity College where Seamus was working, and across College Green the beautiful curved and columned facade of the old House of Parliament were etched magnificently in shades of flame and white against the black night sky. A couple of miles on through the southside suburbs brought us to Donnybrook, where the RTE television and radio complex is located. Ahead of us loomed the enormously high mast, looking every bit like a less elegant version of the Eiffel Tower, which, unlike the Parisian version, would relay the signals of my appearance to my family in Donegal.

We met the producer, John Burns, who took us in to see the studio before bringing us to the hospitality lounge for a drink. I was on cloud nine. Then we met Gillian and her family, it was most heartening to see how well she was then, and that she was a happy normal little girl who could move about without coughing or running out of breath. There was a real buzz, of excitement about the place and for me this atmosphere of joy defies description. In a short while Cathy and I were ushered down to the studio as the audience were being 'warmed up' before the live show commenced. Martine had to remain in the lounge from where she viewed the show on a monitor.

Before going live, a comedian entertained us all with hilarious impressions of our favourite television personalties, including Pat Kenny himself. Broadcasting commenced after *The Nine O'Clock News*, when each and every one of us had to be vigilant against pursuing our undainty little habits like nose picking, in case the camera caught us unaware. The first features to come on included a pair of gigantic Sumo wrestlers who carried Pat into the studio, Sebastian Coe and his wife, a folk music group, and an exceedingly forthright lady singer who not alone stood on Pat's toe, but tried to make love to him on the air! The show, thus far, was entirely light-hearted and fun. I was laughing along with everyone else, and was completely relaxed. Then, all of a sudden Pat announced that he had a more serious topic to discuss. My heart beat faster as he introduced Gillian and Veronica Staunton, for I knew my time to speak would come very soon.

Pat interviewed mother and daughter at length about their experiences. Veronica argued strongly that heart and lung transplantation should be available in Ireland. She encouragingly told of the vast improvement in Gillian's health and lifestyle, evidenced by the strong, happy little girl beside her. Looking at her then, no-one could suspect that she would no longer be with us two years later. The contrast was shown in a flashback from a video made prior to Gillian's operation, when she appeared in the audience, just as I was doing. Apparently, only six weeks after that appearance she received her new heart and lungs! My own, old heart beat faster still at the thought that this could happen for me too, with a bit of luck! Veronica's husband and I, by coincidence, shared the same christian name, and when Pat gave mention to him being in the audience the camera, in error, focussed on me for a moment.

"We have someone here in our studio audience who is waiting for a heart and lung transplant" – Pat's words cued the camera to zoom in on yours truly – "His name is Brendan McLoughlin..." I was just recovering from an attack of wheezing, and words came to me with difficulty. There was only a minute and some seconds to say what I could, so I spoke of how I had just recently been diagnosed as having cystic cibrosis. "Just recently?" Pat questioned how I had been waiting on the dormant Irish list but would soon, hopefully, be going over to England for assessment – "To Harefield?" asked Pat – I told him it would be Newcastle. I was thrilled to embarrass Cathy by drawing attention to 'my nurse'. The floor manager then gave me the signal to hush as Pat turned back to his guests on the platform, but I ignored it. There was no way that I had finished speaking yet. I went on to say hello to my mother in Donegal, to thank all the staff in James Connolly Memorial, and to say thanks to...! At this point I was finally silenced as the camera wung back around to Pat. Poor old Martine and Martin were left out of it against my good intentions.

After the curtain fell on *Kenny Live* one of the camera operators gave me a little tour of RTE. I actually got sitting in Gay Byrne's seat in Studio One, where he hosts his much celebrated Friday night *Late Late Show.* While seated in 'Gaybo's chair I had a copious coughing fit, fortunately the *Late Late* didn't have to be cancelled on 22nd November due to presenter going down with mystery bug.

Being counted among the V.I.P.s present, and chuffed at that, I was ushered, along with Cathy and Martine, into the bar where all the guests, entertainers and their associates enjoy conviviality and drinks on the house. Now that it was all over I could really let my hair down, and did so by relieving RTE of an uncounted number of bottles of Guinness. Finally I had the honour and pleasure of receiving a gift of the first signed copy of Gillian's book. I had dearly hoped to reciprocate by presenting her with a copy of this book. But that wasn't to be.

14

NOW AND FOREVER

On Friday 22nd November, a week after my appearance on *Kenny Live*, Martine arrived to find me transformed in mood. "I'm for England" I told her. I explained to my delighted friend that Dr. Burke had received word from Freeman Hospital in Newcastle concerning arrangements for my assessment; I was booked in for Monday morning! I concentrated all my efforts on getting well enough to take the flight to Britain, only three days ahead. Mother would accompany me, helping to take on board the case full of details and information that the transplant team had in store for us.

The weekend flew like a bullet from a gun. Over the past while, time had crawled like a snake, ready to strike the moment to live or the moment to die. This assessment was going to be a decisive thing, for I was well aware that I might be found unsuitable for surgery. Still, I thought positively, I was going to keep moving forward until I was stopped by something beyond my reckoning. On the auspicious Monday morning, Mother and I were transported from Blanchardstown to Dublin Airport by ambulance. We were stunned by the sheer size and business of an international airport. Mother couldn't believe that something the size of the jumbo jets parked on the tarmac could ever get off the ground. Our plane had a Saab propeller, the same as the one we had witnessed landing on a training flight in Sligo. It was very smart looking, a bit like a scaled-up version of the tiny little aircraft I'd flown in. However, things didn't get off to a good start. We were on cloud nine, but still firmly on the ground taxiing out for taking-off when one of the engines developed a problem. This little incident necessitated a return to the departure lounge, where we spent almost two hours wondering if the repairs would hold out for the trip across the Irish sea!

When we finally got off the ground Mother was too excited to take note of the fact that she was airbound for the first time in her life; she was too preoccupied with her thoughts of all that had happened, and all that lay ahead in my life. The hostess helped us celebrate our first big flight by giving us champagne, it was a lot sweeter than what I was used to and very enjoyable. We were in the front row, a bottle of oxygen at my feet, and a clear view of the pilot's head through the cockpit door which was left open throughout our flight. It was strange to have clouds below us for a change, they appeared to be stationary which gave the impression that our craft was floating motionless in a land of cotton wool. In fact we hurtled through the air at hundreds of miles per hour towards a final hope. I had to quickly gather my wandering thoughts as the pilot announced that we were about to land; it seemed to have taken no time and I was a little disorientated as we were whisked away to the hospital.

Strange accents and friendly smiles greeted us in Freemans. It was straight to business with weighings, measurements, ultrasound investigations, and, of course, the dreaded samples. I was tagged and labelled and felt right at home! I was under the care of Dr. Paul Corris, head of the transplant team. Of course I spoke incessantly to everyone and explained where the accent was from. One girl was also hoping for a transplant like mine, I was later to learn that she was unsuitable. She returned home to live out the days remaining to her. I didn't actually meet her, but I wouldn't care to imagine what she and her family must have gone through. Another lad waiting for a heart swop was successful, and is doing well. It was a lottery of life and now it was my turn, my chance to spin the wheel, where would it land? I had to try and put aside serious thinking for a few days, and enjoy the possibilities that were open to me.

I was in the highly sophisticated cardiothoracic centre, where here, there and everywhere lay emergency call-buttons to summon medical assistance should it be required. One slightly embarrassing situation resulted from my ignorance concerning the location of one of these buttons. I left Mother to read her magazine for a few minutes as I went into the bathroom which was attached to the ward. Suddenly, from our respective positions (mine a rather compromising one) we both heard alarm bells. Mother saw a red light flashing over my door and two nurses approaching swiftly. I was just in the process of pulling up my underpants when they they invaded my privacy, I assured them I was quite able to do that all on my own. Apparently, some part of my anatomy had come in contact with a panic button located beside the toilet seat. I wouldn't mind but Mother's devilish laughter made sure to focus the entire ward's attention on what had happened!

The week was up in a flash, it had been so full that I still can't separate the days in my memory, except the day I was given the news, my nemesis. My left lung was rotten and had never actually grown, very familiar news. But this meant that my body had developed out of shape, it was slightly twisted and bigger on the right. In short, it could never accommodate a new set of bellows; a heart and lung transplant was not an option for me, surprising in view of the fact that I had been assessed as a suitable candidate about two years previously, in Ireland. I guess my insides must have altered shape in the interim. However, all was not lost; those brilliant surgeons had another card to play, an operation whereby a single lung would be put in, in place of what I was living on. It would be more breathing space than I've ever had, which could only be an improvement. Also, the operation would not necessitate cutting the sternum as the doctors would work in through both sides of the abdomen.

We flew back to Dublin digesting all that had happened and wondering what the reactions would be. Most people had never heard of this pioneering surgery (prior to this, even I had understood it was not feasible) and we discovered that I was the first Irish patient to await it. Another media angle for Martine and Martin! They were very surprised at the news and after taking little time to come to terms with yet another game plan, they were delighted. I was in with a chance after all. Friday 13th proved lucky, I received final confirmation that I was on the British transplant list. After all the confusion and red herrings this was finally it. All I had to do was keep breathing and wait.

Back to hospital life, I read about heart and lung transplantee, Karl Wade who was doing very well, four years after his operation. This man is a beacon to us all, looking like any fine, fit, young fellow, grinning out from an article in *Woman's Way*, assuring us by his vitality that it is all worthwhile. Karl, we read, indulges in all kinds of sport, including abseiling, of all things. When I get my new part, I can just picture myself swiftly descending the rocks and cliffs of Donegal with the aid of a rope ... or can I? I hoped that the articles about me would have as good an effect in encouraging others to offer organs for donation.

Christmas was drawing near and I wondered if I'd be home for the festivity. It was a close thing, but Dr. Burke thought it would do me good to experience normal life again. Armed with potions and pills I got home on December 21st. To me, the council townhouse was still a new experience as I had only spent a week living there since the family moved in the previous September. Ironically, I could not afford to go outdoors, to take advantage of the tempting convenience of Jackson's Disco or the pubs which were a stone's throw away. To tell the truth, I hadn't the energy, and hence the desire, to venture out. In fact, being home made me realise just how little quality of life I had left.

A nice Christmas present was the front page spread in *The Evening Press* with the headline: 'LUNG SWOP TO BE FIRST IN IRELAND'. I'm not too sure about the validity of the claim, but it certainly put my name in a few more memories and got people thinking about organ donations again. However, bad news was to follow; little Wayne Tumelty, a seven-year-old C.F. patient who was awaiting a donor, died on 5th January. His publicity had coincided with mine much of the way. It was heartbreaking to think that all his bravery had not been enough. I only know that he and his family brought awareness to thousands of people which someday will save lives. Perhaps my life. He will not be forgotten.

When I was re-admitted in the new year I was quite ill. It had not been a good holiday; most of it spent huddled by an oxygen bottle. I was put on treatment for a growing infection and thankfully responded well. The news on 24th of January 1992 that I was high on the transplant list made me determined to stay well. I am as well as can be expected they say. In a strange sort of way, though chained to a bed and a bottle of air, I am better than I ever was. I am a prisoner about to be set free.

15

FIT TO SURVIVE

I can see the daily, the hourly changes in the weather, their impact on the world around me. I can think of the dirty rainclouds that dull the beautiful countryside of Donegal, or I can see the magnificent sweeps of light that bring to life the colours of nature that lie dormant in the landscape. If I am patient and let time pass I will see that a year of seasons has gone by, bringing with it changes over which I have no control. There are so many things which are totally out of my hands, including the existence of my illness. I cannot afford to let these things get me down, for if I did I could sink so low in spirit that the life force that's in me could drain out, like sap from a dead tree. Then I would be no use to myself or anyone else. Because of the respect I have for my life and myself, I have already gone past my 'live to' date a couple of times.

People come in all forms, shapes and sizes, all colours and hues of personality. I stand out among them because I am different. Most noticeable is my small stature and slight build, my distressing cough (in this context I mean distressing to listen to) and my overall gaunt appearance. People around me respond differently. A few individuals have been incredibly cruel, fortunately only a few. One remark I will never forget as long as I live was uttered by my father, "Take that, you humpy dying bastard." He had just stuck a firelighter into my mouth, his mind responding in its obscene way to a large intake of alcohol. I don't remember this with any sense of self pity, the loss was not mine, here, but my father's, as he had let himself down. Some people jeer me in discos, one lady told my mother that someone like me shouldn't be allowed to swim in public. I presume that the sight of my beautiful body was too much for her. Needless to say she received a colourful reply from my mother and I enjoyed my swim.

These bad times are as significant as I let them be and compared to the attitude of those who care for, and love me, their only impact is to make the good times seem better. What can I do when something tries to get me down? I can't physically afford to get depressed or worry so the attitude I've developed is a healthy one; if I don't like it and can do nothing to alter it, I ignore the thing 'til it goes away. Even bad things come to an end sometime!

I have great power to make life better for myself, inestimable power. There is an enormous amount of good will in many people and it is the likes of my 'unfortunate' self who bring it out in them. I have to realise that everybody is only human, and that I could easily depress them if I sported an unhappy face too often. If I am feeling physically wretched and a friend complains of having a head cold, I can't turn around and say, "Well, that's a wee bit like how I feel at the best of times." You just can't lie back and let the good people take care of you, it is vital to offer them more of yourself than just your illness. As the reader has come to know, there is much more to my life than health problems.

I see some young and vigorous people around me with seemingly everything going for them, and yet they seem to live a tortured existence. They won't or cannot, say what's going on in their minds. Maybe they have something serious bothering them, but I don't know about it unless they tell me. I respect their privacy as long as they don't pull the curtains across innocent windows into the bargain. I will reach out to anyone who knows where to find the faintest smile, even in the deepest recesses of their pocket. Depression is infectious; it can only be overcome through allowing others access to you. A bleak and hostile outlook on the world can only destroy an individual. Someone may be able to help, and in the long term the sufferer may be able to help others.

I love going to dances even though I don't always find someone to dance with. There is always something to be gained just by being there. I come away with a sense of having been exposed to the social scene which is part of any extrovert young person's life. Whenever an opportunity to mix with other people, strangers and friends alike, presents itself, I take it. Everybody's friends were once their strangers!

I hope I can be excused for pontificating a little but I want you to know how I came to be as I am. I have told you the story of a life that has been a profound learning experience. If you have to struggle to live, then by God you appreciate every minute and you cringe when you see what people around you are doing to hurt themselves.

I exercise plenty, in order to be 'fit' to survive. It requires constant vigil to keep my spirits up, a great deal of effort that pays dividends. I have the love of my Mother, my sisters and brothers, and my close friends. I have the goodwill shown to me by countless numbers of people. So many people either need or want me to survive that I owe it to them to fight through any barriers that might come my way. I am determined to survive, even in the darkest hours of a long night. Day will break and when it does I wonder what the dawn will hold for me. I look to the future with a hint of curiosity. It is a little daring because my book tells me to take things one day at a time.

I have always wanted to learn to drive a car, and to own one. A few years ago, I was refused the tax exemption for disabled drivers. Even if I won a million pounds in the National Lottery I couldn't possibly drive a vehicle in my present condition. When I overcome the final major obstacle to my survival I will surely find the means, some day, to have myself behind the wheel of even the most modest motor. I am almost as impatient to achieve this goal as I am to get well, and come dawn I see myself becoming more ambitious in this respect. It is a step towards gaining independence whilst I rehabilitate to becoming a 'normal, average person'. There are many more places in Ireland I want to see, many places I want to revisit on my own accord. I could take Mother out for the odd spin. And when the mood takes me I could visit my friends, in Dublin, without referring to bus timetables. The only time, thus far, I have seen them in their native city has been at Blanchardstown Hospital.

Regarding more exotic ambitions, my intention is to experience further travels by light aircraft. Wherever I find myself, whenever there's a little spare cash in the pocket, I will locate the nearest Aero Club and treat myself to a joyflight. I didn't realise, until recently in Sligo, how easy it is to arrange this little treat. And when I'm not circling the neighbourhood of an aerodrome in a two-seater aircraft, maybe I will find myself travelling further afield in something a little more substantial. Instead of merely constructing a map of the world out of jigsaw pieces, I might construct real travel plans and take a jumbo jet to the USA and back!

My one great hope is that some day I will get married. I would preferably not like to live the life of a bachelor, coming home to an empty dwelling with no special person to share my thoughts with. I have grown up with family all around me, it's the life I know and love. I think most people are made to have companions, it's not natural to be alone and it's bad to be lonely. Whatever happens, I will put in the effort to keep on good terms with my friends. I almost believe that people choose to be lonely, they choose by closing themselves off, by turning their heads, by constantly asking, "Is this all?"

The fact that my father is an alcoholic and is separated from us and has acted as if he hates us has painted it all in black and white. I can see so clearly what he has lost, I can't blame him. People are moulded by their experiences, these experiences and their own intelligence give them the ability to choose. Perhaps my father did not have my choices. I can see how lucky I am, in a sense, to have had the chance to learn to value all I have. Now I need a chance, time, to put my learning into practice. No matter what happens my life has not been wasted, I have kept a record.

There is plenty more I would like to write about that has happened around me, and maybe God will give me the chance. I have no formal education, but life has taught me more than any certificate could testify to. Neither have I any particular qualification for obtaining employment, but if I have to join the dole queue, I have my ambition: to write novels. There are so many unemployed people in Ireland, and indeed overseas, who hold Curriculum Vitaes as long as my medical record, that I wonder if a career opportunity will come my way. But surprises are many if faith is forthcoming and you have the determination to leave no stone unturned.

When I am able to stand on my own two feet, the most significant change will lie in the relationship between my mother and myself. Now, as an adult man I am as dependent on her as if I were a young child. Reciprocally, her whole existence revolves around my welfare. We are both each other's best friend, it is not a situation of Mama Bear and Baby Bear as might impress the reader. Neither of us has anything to hide from the other, and what one suggests the other finds agreeable. We are both of the same mind that life is too precious for bad feelings to rule the day. As long as we are both alive we will always be best friends, but I sometimes wonder how hard it will be for her to adjust to my growing independence. I know she would never try to hang on to me, even though she might experience mixed emotions. One thing is certain, the ultimate goal for her is that I get better.

I know that death as a result of my disease is not an inevitability. I can survive and I have every intention of doing so. I have had an army of goodwill and good deeds behind me, the time is nearing when I can give something in return. At the moment I can just keep my lips above the waterline and keep on swimming. Doctors, nurses, my mother and family, priests, media, friends, we are an army. Since I was told, "six months to live" we have been fighting my battle to survive, and have pushed that date back again and again. Let this book be my thanks to them.

Please God, day break.

EPILOGUE

THE STORM – THE RAINBOW

With the assistance of my family and friends, I reconstruct the final weeks of torment and despair, the endless days of hovering between panic attacks and nothingness that characterised what I then believed to be my last days on earth. In truth I'd prefer not to remember the harrowing tale I now recount.

First, let me tell you that a few weeks ago (as I write today), the best thing in my life happened. It will take time for me to fully appreciate that I am on the road to what I hope will be reasonable health, health such as I've never enjoyed in all my twenty-five years of life. Already I feel in fairly good shape after my recent lung transplant. It is so hard to believe I can talk again after more than ten weeks of silence, that I can breathe without a struggle, that I can delight in eating real food, that ...

Over two months of hell which began on 28th May 1992 when I was put on a life support machine in the intensive care unit at Blanchardstown Hospital in Dublin have now passed. The events which led up to this devastation began shortly before my twenty-fifth birthday when I was brought to Letterkenny Hospital with another bout of the all too familiar pneumonia. I was used to believing that after a few weeks I would come around again, back to what was normal for me. Maybe a bit worse for wear, I could expect a further slight deterioration, but that was part of my illness. I was just ripe for a change of lung.

This is not the way things turned out. Dr. Bannon, my consultant at Letterkenny, transferred me back down to his colleague, Dr. Conor Burke, in Blanchardstown. I had been due for another session of antibiotic therapy there anyway, so I hadn't any great inkling that my cystic fibrosis was reaching its final stage. Admittedly, the day I arrived at the hospital I was feeling pretty miserable, but then I invariably did after travelling that distance in an ambulance. Usually the next day I'd feel on the mend again, but this time I did not. I felt a lot worse.

Dr. Burke casually talked to me about the intensive care unit (I.C.U.) as if it were somewhere I might consider going for a little rest, with the constant attention of nurses to keep me company. In fact, he was deeply concerned about my condition, and was getting me used to the idea of what he undoubtedly knew lay ahead. Yes, I was gasping for each breathful of oxygen and I felt very insecure. By evening I felt even more insecure as I found myself occupying a bed in I.C.U., hooked up to an E.C.G. heart monitor. The noise of its "beep, beep, beep," resounded over my head, and I craned my neck to see a cresting illuminated line making mountains across a screen. Some of them wobbled alarmingly. Was I really that bad?

A fresh I.V. was inserted into my arm, through which, among other drugs, heparin flowed. This prevents blood clotting. Then I was given a couple of units of blood because I was very anaemic. That's why I felt so weak, they told me. Maybe the blood would see me right, I thought. Things aren't so bad afterall. I could see the other patients in I.C.U. were very poorly, much worse off than myself. They were on ventilators to keep them breathing. Hissing, sucking, and mechanical sounds filled the room. Some of these patients were making their first steps to recovery after a major operation. Some had taken drug overdoses and quickly recovered from this particular episode. There are different reasons why patients are put on life support. Some die. Most spend a couple of days to a couple of weeks there, before going to wherever they are going.

Dr. Burke talked to me about ventilators. He said they give the lungs a chance to rest when they have earned a rest and that when you're put on one you're sedated, so things don't seem that bad. He was reassuring me, just in case. But in reality he knew that I'd be needing one soon. All this attention, all these doctors and nurses keeping a close eye on me was proving a bit scary, but the new scenario was a novelty that aroused curiosity as much as fear.

Within a day or two, I was back on the ordinary ward in Unit 8 West, visualising recovery in spite of being still quite sick. But this didn't last long either. Mother had gone back home to Donegal, her mind relatively at ease that things were looking better. She phoned me as usual to see how I was. I walked down the corridor to pick up the phone, my head reeling with dizziness. I gasped a quick 'hello' and instructed her to do all the talking. It was hard to concentrate on what she was saying. However, I did hear her telling me to call assistance from the next person who passed my way. It was a brief conversation, which must have saved some on the phone bill. Two nurses supported me into a wheelchair as my world turned black.

I was rushed back to I.C.U. The sedating drug, Hypnovel, was pumped through my I.V., and the next thing I became aware of was a big tube going down my throat, connecting my airways to a ventilator. This was to be my life support for the next ten weeks. But I was only partially aware of my predicament, as I drifted in and out of consciousness between top-ups of sedation. My temperature was soaring, and Dr. Burke warned my mother that I might not make it through the next few days; it was very much 'touch and go'.

I was aware of people coming in to see me, I recognized familiar voices. Though it was almost impossible to open my eyes, I got the occasional glimpse of hazy figures looking down on me pitifully. I could neither speak nor move myself about in the bed. People held my hand, and I'd acknowledge them by moving my fingers in their palms. Mother was there, almost constantly, it seemed and a priest who knew me very well called in quite often too. My Dublin friends, Martine and Martin, were eventually allowed in. Nobody knew quite what to say to me, except that, "It will be worth it all in the end." There was plenty of awkwardly spoken gossip about everyday things that were happening in the outside world, such as talk about the Maastricht Referendum. They were trying their best to keep me in touch with things that had little relevance to me at the time. How everybody held themselves from betraying their strained emotions I do not know. Outside the room, I believe a lot of crying was done.

Towards the weekend my condition stabilised a little, and Mother was advised to take an all important break, back home with the family in Donegal. She was comforted by the knowledge that my friends were keeping a close eye on me, and would keep her informed on my progress, or lack of it. Martine had just returned from a holiday in Portugal, where it had rained all week in contrast to the warm, mellow sunlight which filtered through the windows in the I.C.U. A beautiful summer outside cast still colder shadows on my winter. Both she and Martin found words difficult to come by. They knew I had enough cop-on not to be misled by bland reassurances. Though I could not partake in conversation, they spoke for me, articulating everything they thought must be going through my head, that I could not let out. Positive efforts to relieve my frustration.

My only glimmer of hope now lay in the fact that I was made aware of the possibility of an imminent call to Newcastle for a lung transplant. I felt I was too ill to be able to undergo such major surgery; but, no, I heard evidence that the hospital was on alert for the call. I was to get the next suitable lung that would turn up. There was discussion of staff and transport arrangements, an aeroplane and pilots were on standby.

This wasn't pie in the sky, it was for real, and could happen anytime. Exactly how soon nobody could surmise, but soon it was to be.

It was nigh time the media were prompted into making urgent donor appeals, thought my close circle of friends. My mother did a fairly lengthy interview with Brenda Donoghue and Dave Fanning who'd taken over Gerry Ryan's spot for his holiday period. Brenda had talked with me from this hospital last year, and she was truly shocked to see what had become of me in the meantime. Apparently there was a terrific response from the 2FM listeners, several of whom pledged to donate a lung if this was feasible, which for ethical reasons it was not. A most wondrous gesture. My mother had asked the surgeon this same question, could he use one of her lungs for me? No, the risk to her life would be too great, no doctor could undertake that responsibility.

Martine and Martin brought my mother on a tour of the Dublin based newspapers, and when that was completed they made phone calls and sent faxed press releases to places outside of the city, including the U.K. From Donegal, my sister Frances spoke on 98FM news, "If he doesn't get a donor soon he'll die, like he can't live the way he is, ... he will die." Brief and to the point, I'd say. She hadn't actually seen me in my present state yet, none of my brothers and sisters had. Mother didn't want them distraught by having to return home to work with that image on their minds. And they thought that if I were to die they wished to remember me the way I was.

An RTE camera crew came into I.C.U. to take some footage and use it to contrast with that taken over a year ago for the television news. I was keeping news correspondent, George Devlin busy, and once again the newspapers filled with headlines such as:'DAYS TO LIVE'. Martine and Martin were to joke later that I had almost embarrassed them by living on; of course they were glad to be abashed! The point of all this media attention lies in the fact that so few lungs are donated. People who think of donating think in terms of the kidneys, eyes, liver and heart, only a small percentage of organ donations are lungs. That is why it is so important to emphasise the need, because the demand completely outweighs the supply. On a personal level this gave me some hope, it also gave my family and friends the feeling that they were doing something concrete to help save my life.

A week after I was put on the ventilator it was decided that I should undergo a tracheotomy, whereby a surgical opening is made through the neck in order to place the air delivery tube directly into my windpipe. In this way my mouth and head would be free and sedation could be reduced to such an extent that I'd be more in tune with the world, though I'd still be unable to speak as the voice box is by-passed. Long-term artificial ventilation patients have this done routinely since complete immobility is not conducive to remaining alive for very long, especially with diseased lungs or circulation. This was the first bit of real surgery I'd ever undergone, and by God it was sore. As I came around from the anaesthetic to a fuller alertness than hitherto, I started to squirm and writhe in response to the cutting, searing discomfort in my neck and lower throat region. I continually asked the nurses to adjust the position of the tracheotomy tube, but no position proved comfortable in a freshly punctured neck. Shots of morphine gave relief from the pain which abated considerably once my flesh healed. I know I could have tolerated it better if it had been a curative procedure, if it was a means to an end.

At least I could sit up now, I could see things. I was able to communicate through writing, but this was a big effort to my weakened hand. People learned to lip read me to some extent. Some were better at it than others. Martin, who is well versed in Sign Language, had in the past tried to encourage me to learn it, (thinking ahead to a time like this). But I never had the energy or concentration to learn such an involved skill. Anyway, it seems to require a lot of dexterity of fingers and both arms, and I was tied up with tubes and lacking vitality. Who can tell, maybe if I'd been in constant practice it would have worked out?

Over the next few days, after the tracheotomy, my two friends were delighted to see some of their old Brendan re-emerging. I was adapting to my new prison. Most of the I.C.U. nurses hadn't known me before, and were now meeting me for the first time. I asked for the television, which was placed promptly beside my bed, and saw myself on the news. What a sorry state I looked! When my friends were present I'd write notes which might need to be passed on to the nurses, for requests, such as the bedpan. Martine, being the divil she is, made up of a couple of notes having forged my handwriting, and there was damned all I could do to stop her, or stop the nurses taking them seriously. One such message read, "I would like a pint of Guinness and then a brandy and soda, one piece of ice." The nurse thought fit to reply, "Brendan, where do you think you are, at the Greyhound?" All I could do was mouth, "Bitch" in revenge, and pinch her arm. Martin was no better, he had a habit of tickling my exposed feet, but then he'd move back before I could kick him.

In due course, I was allowed the odd glass of Guinness, which contained some nourishment, and the odd little sup of brandy which perked me up a bit. I had survived the initial crisis; the antibiotics were managing to keep a check on the infection which was still producing gargantuan amounts of purulent and sometimes bloody sputum in my almost defunct lungs. At fairly short intervals throughout the day this mucus clogged my trachea tube and had to be removed by suction, which was a quick but distressing procedure.

All the time I was wishing and hoping that I could be taken off the ventilator and allowed to speak. Indeed, it is preferred that prospective transplant patients avoid being put on a ventilator if at all possible, since the breathing muscles go into decline if they're not in use. Any attempts to let me breathe on my own were to no avail. I just couldn't take breaths deep enough to sustain a viable level of oxygen in my blood. Every day the machine would need to be disconnected for a couple of minutes whilst routine maintenance was performed, such as changing the humidifying water, and clearing the condensation which built up in the elephant trunk plastic tubes. To me they looked like an elephant's trunk, and my friends called the water container my goldfish bowl.

The place, in fact, was becoming very much like a zoo. Martin brought in, as an extra visitor, his one-eyed stuffed elephant whom he named 'Clarence'. Clarence was to be treated with deference and dignity, and was not supposed to be thrown about my bed like a rubber ball! Martine's life-size Flamingo, alias a nightdress holder, tended to maintain a carefree leggy poise no matter what way he was treated; always the glib smirk on his face. More permanent residents arrived one by one, each sitting on the end of my bed or hanging from my I.V. stand. The orderlies were responsible for my growing family of cuddly toys, of all sizes, shapes and colours.

Many of the other patients, most of whom came and went having recovered from their critical phases, bore their ordeals with remarkable good humour and fortitude. I liked to keep an eye on them, and if I thought that a heart monitor looked to me as if it showed trouble I'd bang my drinking glass to alert the nurses. One old lady in the next bed proved to be quite amusing. She thought she was in a hotel, and threatened to complain to the management about the room service. She was also quite displeased that a football match played by her home county hadn't been televised; had this hotel got something against Kildare? It was nice to see that she recovered from a serious operation as she waved goodbye to her 'boyfriend', an elderly gentleman across the room.

Yes, most patients came and went, but I was still there. It was obvious I would have to remain like this until my transplant. A couple of weeks in this situation seems an awfully long time, and I had no guarantee that the infection would not return with a vengence and overwhelm my frail body. There was every likelihood I might not make it as far as Newcastle. That place seemed a long way away. At first I hearkened to every ringing of the phone, and watched carefully the nurses' expressions which might give me a clue that the all important call had come through. Then I gave up bothering to notice. Just another message about blood test results or bedpans or something.

Every day brought more of the same nothingness. I wasn't even on the inside looking out. I was just on the inside. I couldn't get out of the bed and enjoy the interesting views from the window of the activity below at the hospital entrance, or the verdant panorama of the hospital grounds. Visitors could have ceased trying to involve me in conversation about their daily lives, but they didn't, not yet. I was still, to some extent, pretending to be interested. All I really counted on now was being called to Newcastle, whenever that would come about.

Then, out of the blue, it happened. Mother had just gone down for her evening meal to Unit 8 West. She often dined with a friend of ours, a well-experienced patient named Flo. A lady of some character, Flo had borrowed my pen and was refusing to give it back until I was able to walk in and claim it from her. She and Mother used to attend morning Mass in the chapel, both praying hard and furiously for my intentions. Flo wasn't let visit me, but she said that she could sense my anger. She said that I'd survive by being mad at myself, and she was right.

A few other folks thought my mother was building up her hopes too much, they believed I was too far down the road to be saved. However, Mother wouldn't hear of this talk, she had to keep fighting the battle. Unless death finally had the victory, she would never surrender. My mother is a very persistent lady, and had been keeping in regular touch with Newcastle. However, today she was quite upset that last night Freeman Hospital had discouraged her from calling them that often.

She had got one mouthful of her meal past her lips when she was told to return to I.C.U., as the call had come through. Quite naturally she was very excited, and somewhat hassled. There was some quick last second packing to be done and a couple of phone calls to be made. For my part, I couldn't believe my luck. Nothing could go wrong now. Of course, I was ever so nervous, this was such a big step to take. Whatever the risks, I had enormous hopes of surviving the operation. I asked not to be put asleep for the journey so as to be able to savour every moment.

Two doctors, two nurses, my mother, myself, and a portable ventilator; we all made headway down the corridor, into the lift, through the hall and out into the fresh air. The beginning of my journey into the living world.

A waiting ambulance rushed me to Baldonnell Military Aerodrome, where a Beechcraft Aeroplane was ready on the apron, courtesy of the Irish Air Corps. Everything ran as smooth as clockwork. The pilots and

Army personnel seemed pleased with their rather unusual mission. There was no waiting around, Air Traffic Control gave us an immediate clearance for departure, and away we went. Mother sat in the back seat, which she learned served the dual function of being the toilet; so there was Mother, sitting on the bog for the hour it took us to get across!

Another ambulance waited on the tarmac at Newcastle International Airport. The journey was slightly smoother on English roads. Seven miles to Freeman Hospital took minutes to cover. Then into the clean, bright and calm atmosphere of the cardiothoracic centre, and up to the first floor where Ward 27A, the transplant unit, lies. Preparations begin, and I am waiting. It is Wednesday 24th June, 8.00 p.m. The I.C.U. in Dublin was just over two hours ago and yet a million years past. Nothing can go wrong now.

Bit it did, it went very wrong. The drama, ending at midnight, never reached the second act. I am left to sleep in solitude for several hours, but I am not asleep. Mother is going through her own grief in a separate room. The donor lung was found to be unsuitable. I hadn't reckoned on this happening to me; was I stupid or what?

Two days later a very depressed Brendan arrived back to his prison cell in Dublin. They kept me very sedated most of the time, and that suited me fine. I didn't want to know anything, or anyone.

Mother tried to get me to work through my emotions, and she succeeded temporarily in having me explode on paper. This is what I wrote, verbatim:

I don't know what it is, tired,
I can't speak,
Things feel bad inside me,
Feel like crying,
My world is turned upside down.

I hate what happened –
It should have gone right.
Makes me mad,
I don't want to die,
Want to cry,
You cry, then I will cry –
Keep it up.

Don't want to sleep all the time,
Want help to fight.

Let down like someone closed
a door on my face.
I am feeling sick, O.K.?
Not being able to cope with it.
My world fell apart.

I couldn't believe it,
Angry and disappointed,
I feel sick inside
And also, sadness
Because I am so strong, and
It isn't expected.

I am still feeling (that way)
and I don't know why.
Should be able to bounce back
up again.
They are listening but I am not
responding.
It's a feeling,
I am feeling bad,
Don't know,
Feeling tired,
Feel tired and sick.

I am nervous,
I am nervous,
I am still nervous,

I can't talk about how I feel because
I am unable ... I feel let down
badly and no one will listen.
Because I can't speak they think that
I am making it up and I should
not have those kind of feelings.

I feel like a fool not being able to
cope with such a simple thing as
being turned down. I thought you
would not understand because I
was so strong.
That is why I feel nervous, because
I can't talk about it. I feel unable
to cry and I don't know why.

When I got off the plane in England
I felt nothing could go wrong and
at half-passt twelve everything
dropped. I felt that people
would think I was mad and would
not help me anymore because
I was a let-down.

I can't cope with the fact that I
was turned down,
I feel sick all over.

They're going to let me sleep now.

A few hours after I'd written this note, Martin and Martine came in to visit, only to find me asleep. From this point on Hypnovel was the only friend I wanted to know, and as the reader can see I clearly hated my change in disposition. My friends were shocked to read about my feelings because they had never known me to be like this before. Depression had finally taken hold and would not release me until after my transplant. With my consent, our good friend from *The Donegal Democrat*, Chris Ashmore published my notes for the people of my native county to read. That was it, I thought, my chance had come and gone.

The nurses were upset too. The two girls who were in charge of me on the flight to Newcastle heard the bad news after arriving back in Dublin on their scheduled Aer Lingus plane. They'd phoned Blanchardstown to say they'd be coming back to work shortly by taxi when their colleagues told them they'd be seeing me again, very soon. Both of them cried, they confessed to Martin and Martine.

Mother did a further interview with Dave Fanning, this time encouraged by a pre-arranged phone-in by Michael Collins from Sligo, who underwent a successful heart and lung transplant two years previously. A few days later Michael came in to see me and empathised with all I was going through, though his situation had been slightly different.

The Sligo connection continued when Martin came in a day later with his camcorder, which, plugged into my television set, played back the video he'd made of me last summer. Glencar, with its beautiful waterfall, and Parkes Castle by the shore of Lough Gill, and Ben Bulbin, queen of those curiously flat-topped mountains. I looked so good then, so happy in myself. For a moment I was back there, being happy. Now it was time to sleep again.

A mere week and a half had elapsed when it all happened again. Saturday morning, 4th July, 6.00 a.m. This time I didn't believe it and I was right. Being the weekend, Mother was at home in Ballybofey when she got the message. She made a quick dash across Northern Ireland to catch the scheduled Gill Air flight from Belfast Harbour Aerodrome. When in the boarding queue, she was called aside to be told that my second Air Corps mercy mission had been instructed to return to Dublin with me on board. Apparently, there were problems during the removal of the donor lung. This time she just laughed, the whole thing was so ridiculous she couldn't help but see the funny side. I never even got off the plane, but I was clocking up a lot of flying hours!

People said the good thing was that another lung had turned up so soon, and this bode well for the immediate future. Still, the second let-down didn't help me. Things that I would have been thrilled with in the past meant far less to me now, because I was dying when I could have been saved. Flowers, hand-picked by President Mary Robinson, were delivered to me from Aras An Uachtarain; a kind and lovely letter from Bibi Baskin, asking me, 'Not to let the Donegal side down'; a card was sent from the newsroom in RTE. I also received a message from Gillian Staunton, the bright and happy transplant girl I met on *Kenny Live* ; a video recorder lent to me by the Irish Kidney Association; and many, many more kind thoughts and deeds from well-wishers, which I can now look on with due appreciation.

Still more weeks passed, and no sign of another call. Members of my family came to visit and were horrified by the stranger they found. On the surface I had faded physically, that was expected, but I was still hanging on in there. On the inside, there dwelt a tormented mind. I had gone past the stage of being disillusioned by my own apathy, I'd given up explaining the context of my behaviour to myself or others. I was uncomprimising to the needs of my helpers.

Each evening I demanded to be put asleep earlier and earlier. The nurses had a ferocious struggle trying to keep me to stay awake until the set time of 9.00 p.m. It was physically bad for me to sleep too much, my muscles needed to stay in tone.

Martine and Martin would be there, aiding and abetting them, and I would be sorely annoyed with them all. My intellect told me they were doing it for my own good, but if I was going to die anyway where was the good? I suffered episodes of terror and panic; shaking from head to toe. This, and banging my glass on the bedside locker were the only movements that spared me total passive immobility. The priest would be there too, "I'm part of the dreadful conspiracy", he said. They had to treat me with some degree of humour. If they hadn't laughed they'd have cried, and that wouldn't have done me any good. Now the life force had totally drained from me, like sap from a dead tree.

A month had passed since my second aborted call to Newcastle. Less than that amount of time had elapsed from the day I was initially put on life support, to the day I got my first false alarm. And only a week and a half between the two calls. By now I thought I was probably off the list in England. I was more than likely too poorly to survive surgery. For the past week I'd refused all visitors, except my mother whom I barely tolerated being present. Nobody took it personally, because this was not Brendan.

One morning, under the strain of it all, Mother collapsed and ended up in 'Casualty' downstairs. She had been talking to the social worker when she took the turn. Worried that it might be a return of her heart condition, the doctors gave her a thorough examination. No, it was just a bad case of stress, and she was ordered to rest, under supervision, for a few hours. She too had begun to doubt that I was still on call for a transplant.

So did Martine and Martin. Having been turned away from visiting for a fortnight they both thought they smelled a rat. On Monday, August 10th, Martine phoned Martin at work to tell him what she honestly felt the situation must now be. Martin was in full agreement, in fact he was entirely convinced that I had been taken off the transplant waiting list. Then a minor argument erupted. No matter what her feelings, Martine would sustain a one per cent hope, "Damn it, Martin, we could be proved wrong any second".

Martin said he was going to phone my mother, as it was unlike her not to be in contact for so long. He thought she must have found out for definite that I had been taken off the list and was now too disheartened, and upset to talk. He was determined to find out what the hell was going on. It was five weeks since the last lung had turned up, but it seemed like five years.

My mother had just come down from Donegal that day. When she arrived I just told her to go off and get some rest, that I wanted to sleep all day. However, she had someone to talk to when Martin phoned. "It's the worst I ever found him mentally, the way he's been recently, and that's telling you something!" she told my friend. Still she was putting her mind together as to how best to get the inside information concerning my status as a transplant candidate. She thought that maybe the doctors imagined she'd go berserk if she knew the truth, and so they were hiding it from her.

Teatime saw the usual disappearance of Mother from the I.C.U. Not unusually, I refused solid food, resorting instead to a furious gulp of 'Liquisorb' nourishment. I swallowed as fast as I could, so as not to notice I was 'eating'. Mother hadn't even reached the kitchen before being called back. "Brendan wants to see you", a nurse told her. That's not likely, she thought, not unless he's taken very bad or something. I saw her coming in, looking quite frazzled. "What's wrong, Brendan?" she asked. I didn't quite know what was going on myself. Then the news was broken about yet another journey to Newcastle. Of course, I didn't believe 'my luck would be in' this time either. Mother, on the other hand, was quite confidant. "It might be, you know, Brendan, it might be third time lucky". I asked to be sedated for the trip, no more could I enjoy aeroplanes.

This Air Corps plane was bigger than the Beechcraft, so Mother wasn't obliged to sit on the toilet. She was afforded more dignity! We had been called an hour earlier than the first time, and things were happening more rapidly but I was too sedated to appreciate it. A voice said, "You're nearly ready for theatre", then I think I dozed off again.

Meantime, back in Ireland the lines of communication were electric. Everyone was sort of convinced of this 'third time lucky' business. Mother had contacted Martine's home and spoke to Martine's mother who then relayed the message to Martine at work. Martin was in turn contacted by his namesake, and he followed this up with a call to RTE. The media had already been informed by the hospital, but George Devlin, the news correspondent, gave Martin the opportunity to say a few words on the 6.30 p.m. radio news. Bulletins were popping up throughout the evening on all stations, and that was how my father, brothers and sisters, and my friends were all kept informed. As Martin had said on broadcast, "It means for us the waiting has begun again".

At around 10.30 p.m. I was wheeled into theatre. "Right, Brendan, expect to feel a bit strange as you're coming to. Remember, we'll be with you all the time. You're in very good hands with Mr. Dark." Unknown to me, another man was being given the other lung in an adjacent theatre. A busy night for two highly-skilled surgeons. This was really it, then?

Back home in Ireland, the 11.00 p.m. bulletins spelt out the good news, "The operation is going ahead this time". Martin said it felt like Christmas. My family made potful after potful of tea to keep themselves alert.

Mother took root in a small room, not too distant from the action. She knew it was going to be a long, long night, and there was no way she could doze off in her easy chair. Nor could she interest herself in reading the newspapers provided. Her room had a twin next door where a lady called Diane was holding a similar vigil. It was her husband who was receiving the other lung.

Of course, I was oblivious throughout the eight-and-a-half hours it took top surgeon, Mr. Dark, to perform the mammoth surgery.

Internal alterations and re-structuring were needed to allow my new healthy lung to work efficiently as my insides had long since adopted the shape required to get the most out of my rotten lungs. He had to cleanse my tissues of pseudomonas and all the infective bugs that had made their home in me. Maybe he called in Rentokil for assistance? Then he had to do the essential bit; fitting in a nice new lung. He had his work cut out.

On the 8.00 a.m. radio news, Anne Doyle announced that I was in a stable condition, recovering in intensive care. The folks back home were privileged to hear this before Mother did. They had the edge on her by a few minutes. The next few hours would be critical.

In my first hazy awareness I felt little difference from before the operation, except that the air now flowed in and out through my chest more easily. I was still on a ventilator, but it was doing less work, I felt. There was no pain, and I wondered why. I found out that painkiller was being fed directly into my spine like an epidural anaesthetic. I had survived to realise I'd achieved a transplant. And only the day before, we had all lost hope!

During the afternoon Mother was allowed to have a peep at me from behind the glass. To achieve even this much she had to scrub up like the surgeon, and wear freshly laundered theatre attire. This was essential because my environment had to be kept germ-free as I was on heavy immunosuppressive drugs to minimise the very real risk of rejection. She thought I looked absolutely awful, noticing the total absence of colour in my ears. The staff reassured her that this was normal, that my circulation was ticking over at just the right pace for this stage of recovery.

Mother thanked God that we had achieved this much. She couldn't have come to terms with my death if that had occurred before I got even the chance of seeing how I would fare with a donated lung. Medical science was doing all it possibly could do to save my life. If things went wrong now there would be no pondering over 'what could have been'. I was remarkably lucky to have stayed alive so long in that condition. Other cystic fibrosis sufferers like little Wayne Tumelty, and more recently, Tony O'Brien from Dublin, had died waiting.

At 8.00 p.m., just twelve hours after the operation, they took me off the ventilator. It worked, I was breathing on my own for the first time in over ten weeks. This was a remarkable sign of improvement, the first benefit I experienced from the transplant. Obviously, the new lung was much better than the old cystic fibrosis one, now probably being dissected for research if it wasn't too much of a health hazard to the pathologist! I was still on oxygen, of course, this had to be administered for the next couple of weeks.

The next day Mother was allowed more direct contact, and found me looking a lot better. She was startled to hear me speak, having forgotten that my voice still existed. I had already spoken my first words to the nurses, telling them to make sure that my mother got something to eat as she had missed her tea the night of my transplant. At first it wasn't easy talking, and I was instructed not to do too much of it. They must have remembered what a lot I said when I was there the year before, having my assessment.

Over the next few days I began to learn to walk again. I required a lot of physical support at first, and had to take things very slowly. My leg muscles needed a great deal of strengthening after being inactive for so long. I enjoyed good solid meals now, as my appetite was boosted by the cortisone used for immunosuppression. I could choose what I fancied from the quite extensive menu, so there was little left on my plate. I also enjoyed snacking between meals, especially on ice cream.

Six days after surgery I was allowed out of intensive care, and sent to Cubicle 5, one of the single-bedded, self-contained rooms on Ward 27A. I had my own bathroom and television and there was a video player at my disposal, as well as books, games, jigsaws, or whatever else I fancied. The bedclothes were cheerfully patterned in blue and mauve which made a change from regulation white.

There were other heart and lung transplant patients in the rest of the cubicles on the ward. Most were doing very well, including Diane's husband. In fact he was recovering faster than me. He was making journeys up to the kitchen which is shared by doctors, nurses, patients and relatives alike. He had even started using the exercise bikes, that was until he began to feel slightly unwell. I, on the otherhand was still having my good days and my bad days, and I didn't wonder after twenty-five years of illness.

Then Diane's husband became worse. Suffering from massive rejection he had to be brought back to intensive care and put on a ventilator. His transplanted lung collapsed, and now he survived solely on his other, original lung which was poorly effective as it was diseased with emphysema. He didn't survive for long, though. Sadly he was one of the unlucky recipients who suffer uncontrollable rejection. Cyclosporin is an excellent anti-rejection drug, but it can't be guaranteed to work for everyone, nor could all such drugs, compounded in a cocktail.

It was a bit of a shock to us, especially knowing that I had the other half of a breathing system which had been rejected. But I was a different individual with my own immune system, and my prognosis would be a separate thing entirely. We were told I could expect some degree of rejection in the first six weeks, that this was the rule rather than the exception. When I developed a slight temperature one day, rejection was indeed suspected, and a biopsy of lung tissue was immediately ordered to be taken. The practice of tissue testing has contributed greatly to the increasing success rate of lung transplants. Rejection can be pin-pointed accurately, and the appropriate treatment instituted. The result of my biopsy was good, I was almost clear.

My two sisters, Frances and Martina, came over to visit me for a few days. Less than a fortnight after my surgery they found me in a 'mixed' condition, but in general, immensely improved on what I had been back in Dublin. Martine came to see me too, her visit partly coinciding with that of my sisters. Mother badly needed to catch up on shopping. My sisters had brought over some of my clothes, but I would require a tracksuit and trainers for exercise; all the other patients were sporting tracksuits. Pyjamas were for night time only. Now that the girls were over, Mother took the opportunity to go into the city centre and look around the superb shopping centres, arcades and streets of Newcastle. As her sight is pretty bad, the girls were the guide dog she needed to negotiate the transport system, including the highly acclaimed Metro system.

Mother also enjoyed her first night out to a pub in a very long time. She found it hard to let go, to be able to leave her recent troubles behind. With a sense of guilt she asked me if I would be alright for the evening. Quite alright, I assured her, and happy to see her get out. All things being equal, I wouldn't be too long in joining them.

Tons of cards had arrived to Freeman Hospital. From all the people who'd sent me greetings before, and from many, many others. We had great fun trying to identify the senders. Who was Paul Mullen, C.F.I. Sligo? "He was the man who took you up last year on your very first aeroplane ride, remember." C.F.I. stood for Chief Flying Instructor. Ah, yes, of course, I could never forget that! Many of my well-wishers were total strangers, and some of them were local Newcastle people. They had heard about the 'lad from Ireland' on local radio and in *The Northern Echo*. Mother received several offers of help from these kindly and thoughtful 'Geordies'. One lady went as far as coming to the hospital with huge bagfuls of goodies for us. Mother was embarrassed at her generosity, especially when this kind lady arranged repeat visits, apologising if on a certain day she wouldn't be able to come.

A mere three weeks after my lung transplant I was called to speak on RTE radio via the telephone. I think the folks back home who were still drowsy with sleep at 9.00 a.m. quickly came to their senses. Was this Brendan McLoughlin as he is today, right now? Yes it was, and a Brendan who had just taken to stationary cycling in the corridor. Now I was on the move.

The storm had passed, a rainbow was now visible. Dawn had broken.

AFTERWORD

Christmas approaches once again; a year has passed and much has happened. In the space of twelve months we have seen our friend Brendan sink to the very edge of death and wallow for weeks at its door. Through him we saw what it is to be human and stripped of all the trappings which clothe our lives, until nothing is left but instinct, forcing us to cling to the last thread of hope.

The year has changed us too; the sunny days and the rainy days spent in James Connolly Memorial Hospital, all those weeks wondering if we were doing any good at all. The long weeks in intensive care watching Brendan slowly slipping away from us – afraid to hope that he would pull through and afraid not to hope. Brendan has not fully remembered this time, and we are glad of this because he suffered a lot.

We learned much and are still learning from that time. We saw courage from Brendan and the many others whose cases we followed. We learned about death from those who didn't make it. But most of all we will remember hope; that ability when faced with seemingly insurmountable odds to go on believing that somehow for some reason; you're going to survive. Brendan was attached to state of the art technology for longer than anyone believed he could withstand. Nobody knows how he survived that long. He got to the stage where he wouldn't see anyone because he didn't have the mental energy to deal with them. He didn't want friends, he didn't want family, he just needed to be left alone; not to die but to wait. So he out-waited death. He out-hoped almost all of us, and he won.

After Brendan flew home from Newcastle following his transplant, we met him in the same hospital where Martin had first visited him almost two years previously. Then, he had been a chirpy young man full of life and energy. We were to see him waste away over that time until he was the barest of skeletons needing all his breaths pumped into him. Sometimes we wondered if he would be better off dead instead of enduring this terrible suffering. But here he was again, by some miracles, with the light back in his eyes and looking better than we had ever known. You could see the life in him, he was bursting with it. He talked of the plans he had and the things he would do. He chatted away nineteen to the dozen in typical Brendan style, in a way we were shocked, dumbfounded at the change in him. We listened until it was time to leave and then, for the first time for far too long; he walked us to the door.

It has changed us all.

Martin Byrne
Martine Brangan
December 1992